The

Christmas Miracle

of 1914

Thanks

Kannon Graves

The

Christmas Miracle

of 1914

Kannon E. Graves

with

Kathleen Graham-Gandy

Shock Inner Prizes Publishing House
Mount Pleasant, Tennessee

The Christmas Miracle of 1914

Kannon E. Graves
with Kathleen Graham-Gandy

Published by:
Shock Inner Prizes
Publishing House
USA

ISBN: 0-9800811-3-0
ISBN-13: 978-0-9800811-3-8
1. Fiction / Action & Adventure
2. Fiction / Historical

Cover Design: Charles E. Gandy

. ACKNOWLEDGEMENTS

I would like to thank the following:

Mr. Wayne Harris, whom I met at the Giles County Library, for the time he spent with me doing research for WWI Christmas Truce of 1914 facts. I appreciate how he shared his own personal military history and the military history of his family. Thank you, Mr. Wayne, for your service to our country.

The staff at the Giles County historical/genealogy department who helped me with a lot of information on our local service men and women in the Giles County area.

Mr. Rich and the staff at Elkton School for their assistance by allowing Latarious and me to step out of class for photo shoots and their support of my project ("The Book").

Ms. Angela Secrest, Librarian for Riverside Elementary School, Columbia, Tennessee for her gift of two WWI books. These books were invaluable to my research.

Thanks to my Dad who took me to Rippavilla to see a WWI exhibit. We had a great tour guide who gave information about the WWI era that was helpful to this publication.

And, last but not least, I would like to thank my family and friends, and Memaw's friends, who helped to edit this book. Thanks for believing that we could make this happen.

DEDICATION

I want to dedicate this book in memory of Mr. Barnes Preston Lovelace, the grandfather of Mr. Wayne Harris. Mr. Lovelace served in the military from 1917 until his release from active duty in 1925. Mr. Lovelace, who was in the mortar battalion, was the sole survivor of his unit.

I dedicate this book also to the Giles County Veterans, past and present, whose bravery to fight for our country and freedom allowed me to be privileged to write my book due to their selflessness and love of others. We live in a great country.

COVER PHOTO:

The cover photo depicts Latarious Brewer (Leon), my best friend, and this author, Kannon Graves (Sam) as we witnessed the Christmas Truce of 1914, the central theme of this fictional book. Note the brass box that Latarious and I are holding in the picture. It was an original Princess Mary WWI gift to the English military on the frontlines.

« CHAPTER 1 »

Sam tossed the nerf basketball into the air and caught it between his hands. "I'm bored," he sighed loudly. School had been out for less than a week and he was already wishing that he had something to do. He was signed up for basketball camp but that didn't start for another month. He knew that he would be spending some time with his grandparents this summer, but right now he didn't have anything planned.

"Sam." He could hear his mom calling him from the kitchen. He was in his room, lying on the rumpled bed with the covers hanging to the floor. Mom had sent him to his room half an hour ago to make up his bed and pick up his clothes, but he hadn't gotten started on that yet.

"Sam!" Mom yelled again. "We need to leave if we're going to get to the library in time for story hour."

Sam let out a groan. Library? Story Hour? That's just what an eleven year-old wants to do on his summer vacation. Go to the library.

Sam enjoyed learning about history. He watched the History Channel on TV all the time. Some of the stories about World War I and World War II were fascinating. He learned something new each time he watched a show about the two wars. But story time? Oh man, who wants to listen to someone read. Story time is for little kids.

"Coming, Mom!" He shouted as he got off his bed. He tossed the basketball on the dresser, knocking off one of his army men. He would have to pick that up later.

Sam entered the kitchen just as Mom's cellphone rang. He watched her as she listened to the person on the other end of the call. "Well, we were just leaving to go to the library," Mom said into the phone.

Mom listened again. "Okay. We will pick him up on our way. I'm sure he will enjoy the story hour, too." Mom nodded her head as though the other person could see her through the phone. "It is no problem, Anne. We would love for Leon to join us."

Leon was going with them to the story hour? Perfect! Now it would be fun! Leon was always fun to be around.

Sam ran out to the car. "Come on, Mom! We need to hurry if we're going to get there on time!"

Sally Baxter laughed at her son. Just a few moments ago she had to practically drag him out of his room and now that Leon was going with them, well, now *he* was the one in a big hurry. Boys!

Sam jumped in the car and buckled his seat belt. Mom got in and buckled up, too. "Mom, I sure wish Leon still lived next door. Summer would be a lot more fun if he was still here. We could practice basketball more often."

Sally rolled her eyes at her young son and replied, "Sam, I don't think that I could keep up with the two of you. Why don't we plan a sleepover soon?"

Sam was excited about that idea. He looked out the window as his mom drove across town. He wondered what today's story hour would be. He sure hoped it wasn't some baby story! Most of the time the people who read to the kids at the library always chose a story for little kids. He was too old for some of those stories. I mean, he was in middle school now. A story about an airplane would be nice. He was daydreaming about airplanes landing in the street when he felt the car turn right.

There was Leon waiting in the driveway! Anne Webster was standing behind her son with her keys in her hand. Sam's mom rolled down her window. Anne leaned down to the window. "I really appreciate you taking Leon with you, Sally. His grandmother called at the last minute to say she could not watch him this afternoon. You are a lifesaver."

Sally smiled and said, "I honestly don't mind, Anne. Sam is always glad to spend time with Leon. He has been out of school for a week and he is already bored. So it will be good for him to be with Leon this afternoon."

Anne laughed. "Leon is already bored, too! He told me yesterday that he was thinking that he needed to get Sam to come over so they could practice some basketball. They will find any excuse to get together, won't they?"

"That they will," said Sally. Sally waved and then backed out of the driveway.

Sally looked in the rearview mirror. The boys had their heads together as if they were plotting something big. She stopped at a traffic light. As she watched the two boys in the mirror, she studied her young son's face. Samuel (Sam) Baxter had blonde hair with blue eyes and freckles

3

across his nose. His laugh always filled a room with light. Sam had to be moving at all times. It seemed as though he could never sit still for even a few minutes. He was definitely her "active" child. His sister, Mikayla, who was a couple years older than Sam, was a typical teenage girl. She enjoyed being active in cheerleading but she was also more reserved than Sam... she was a teenager with a phone.

Leonardo (Leon) Webster had dark hair with dark brown eyes and an infectious smile. He was Sam's best friend. They had been friends since they were four years old. Leon used to live next door until they moved to a different neighborhood a few years ago. Things hadn't been the same in the old neighborhood since. Leon had an older brother who couldn't be bothered with a younger brother tagging along with him everywhere he went. It was good that Sam and Leon were friends so that they had someone to share basketball and other sports activities with.

Together they made quite the pair. The teachers at school always teased them that they were like the *Bobbsey Twins*...light and dark and always together.

Sam was not your typical eleven-year old. He was thoughtful, kind, considerate of others, and generous with anything he had. He was always doing things for the less fortunate and their elderly neighbors. Just last week he pulled weeds out of Mrs. Scott's flower beds. She wanted to pay him for his work, but Sam refused payment. When he got home he told his mom how Mrs. Scott wanted to pay him. "She is always giving me cookies and lemonade. I told her that was payment enough." Yes, Sam was different, but in a good way.

Leon was a lot like Sam in that he was always thoughtful of others. Leon was quiet to Sam's outgoing personality. That was why they fit so well together.

Leon had to help his mom with her mother. Leon's grandmother was in poor health and Leon and Anne had to clean her house and mow her yard. Leon never complained that he had to do chores for his grandmother when he would rather practice basketball.

Anne and Sally felt blessed to have such sweet boys. Sally sure hoped they would stay that way…especially through their teenage years. They were growing up too fast. But Sally wasn't going to think about that right now. She was going to enjoy each day with them and pray that the teenage years would be easy on all of them.

Sally pulled into the parking lot of the library and parked the car. She turned in her seat and looked at the boys. "Boys, I have errands to run, so I'll be back in two hours to get you."

Sam's eyes widened. "You mean, you aren't coming in with us?"

"You will be fine," his mom told him.

Sam sputtered. "Bu…bu…but, I mean, what if we don't like the story hour? You know how they usually read stories for little kids! If you leave we will be stuck here for the whole two hours!" Sam leaned his forehead into his hands and groaned out loud.

Leon elbowed Sam in the ribs. "It won't be that bad. Come on. If it's a little kid story we just won't listen. I'm sure we can find something to entertain us until Mrs. B. comes back for us."

"Now I don't want you two misbehaving. Mrs. Potts will let me know if you do," Sally said with a grin.

Sally watched as Sam and Leon got out of the car and walked toward the library. Leon was jostling Sam and laughing. Sam just shrugged his shoulders.

As she drove away she was thinking that she didn't have to worry about the boys misbehaving, but she knew she should remind them to behave anyway...just as a precaution.

« CHAPTER 2 »

Sam and Leon walked in the front door of the library. "Sam! Leon! I am so glad to see you today," greeted Mrs. Potts, the librarian. She had short, curly white hair that looked as though it was going in a million different directions. Her glasses, which she wore on a chain around her neck, were hidden behind the stack of books in her arms. It seemed as though she was always searching for her glasses. Even now she patted her head as though trying to find them.

Both boys said "hello" as they looked around to see if any of their friends were at the story hour. They couldn't see anyone they knew.

Mrs. Potts continued talking, "We have a wonderful surprise guest today. It is a gentleman who lives in Kentucky and he is in town visiting with his granddaughter and her family for a few months."

"That's nice," Sam replied, still looking around to see who was in the library.

"You boys go on and find some chairs. There will be others coming in soon. The younger children will be meeting in the play room today so that they will not be a distraction to our special guest."

Sam was glad to hear that the younger kids were going in the play room. That meant that the story hour wasn't for little kids. That was a good sign…he hoped.

Sam and Leon walked into the reading room. Leon jabbed Sam in the ribs (it seemed as though Leon was always poking Sam in the ribs!). "Man, this guy is one OLD Dude! Look at him! He is older than my grandpa!"

"Leon! Not so loud! He will hear you!" Sam scolded him as he grabbed Leon's arm.

A little girl about their age walked over to the boys. "Hi. My name is Sophie. That 'old dude' is my great-grandfather."

Sam blushed and his freckles popped out across his nose as he realized that Sophie had heard Leon's remark.

She was just a tad shorter than Sam. She had curly hair that gleamed like a new copper penny. Like Sam, she had freckles across her nose and cheeks. Her blue eyes sparkled in mischief as she watched them. She enjoyed watching their discomfort at Leon's remark.

Sam stuttered. "Hi. Uh, hi. I am Sam and this is my best friend, Leon."

Leon nodded his head. "Hey, I didn't mean any disrespect about that 'old dude' remark. I was just surprised to see someone that old here. I mean…aw shucks; I'll just shut up now."

Sophie laughed. "That's okay. We celebrated his 90th birthday last week. That *is* old to us! In fact, anyone over *20* is old to us!" Her laughter was sweet and soft, like the sound of tinkling bells.

"But my great-grandfather is in good health and we are so glad that he was able to come visit us. He can't play with me or anything, but I enjoy listening to him. In fact, he has a great sense of humor and tells wonderful stories. I think that y'all will enjoy listening to him today."

"I'm sure that we will enjoy hearing him talk to us. My grandpa likes to talk about when he was young, too. Some of *his* stories are interesting and funny," Sam replied.

A woman came up to Sophie and put her hand on Sophie's shoulder. Sophie looked up at her and smiled. "This is my mother, Beth. My great-grandfather is her grandfather."

The boys nodded "hello" and moved on to their seats. Sam heard a noise at the door. He looked up just as two boys from his class walked through the door.

"Hey Sophie!" Billy shouted with a booming voice. "Long time no see!"

Leon whispered, "Oh man! Why did HE have to show up today? This story hour was looking up for us. I hope he doesn't say anything stupid. He can be such a pain at times."

Sam nodded. Billy was bigger and taller than Sam. In fact, Billy could be a bully at times. He liked to cause trouble for those around him. Even though Billy tried to be a tough guy around school, Sam had heard that he had a rough life at home. Sam tried to be friendly, but Billy usually called him "squirt" or "runt" and would elbow him in the hallway at school. Just last week Billy threatened to stuff him in a locker. Sam tried to avoid him as much as possible, but it was hard to do in their small hallways at Elkton School.

9

"It's time to take your seats everyone," announced Mrs. Potts. Her hands were moving as though she was still looking for her glasses. And there they were…perched on her head.

The seats were arranged in a semi-circle. Sam and Leon sat in seats that were across from the older gentleman. Leon sat on Sam's left. Billy sat two seats down from his right. Sophie sat next to her great-grandfather. The light from the window revealed blonde streaks in her red hair. Sam tried to look above Sophie's head so that he wasn't looking directly at her, but his eyes kept catching hers. She smiled at him. Sam blushed, gave her a half-smile, and looked away.

Mrs. Potts walked up to stand behind the older gentleman. She began speaking, "Children, I am so glad that you are here today. I am so excited about our guest. I want to introduce you to Mr. Theodore (Teddy) Sampson. He is here today to talk about his father, McFerrin Sampson. Now boys and girls, please give your full attention and respect to Mr. Teddy today. I know that you're going to enjoy some of the things he tells you about his father and some of the battles he witnessed in World War I. We are so blessed to have someone that can tell us more about that era."

Sam sat up straighter in his chair. World War I? He enjoyed watching the History Channel about World War I. Maybe today's reading hour won't be so bad after all. He caught himself smiling and looking at Sophie.

Leon groaned inwardly. He didn't care much for history. Now if it was someone talking about basketball, well, Leon could listen all day. But history? Oh, man, this story hour was going to be so boring.

~~~

Billy looked at Sam and winked. Then he took a piece of paper from his pocket, rolled it up, leaned back in his chair and threw the paper wad at Sophie's head. It landed in her hair. Billy watched for her reaction but she just sat listening to the old man speak. Billy felt in his pockets for something with a little more weight to it so she would feel the "thump" as it landed on her head.

He pulled out a penny and held it up for Sam to see. Once again, he leaned back in his chair and tossed the penny toward Sophie. Billy's eyes widened as he realized that he had missed his mark and the penny fell at her mother's feet. Sophie's mother glanced down at the penny. She looked up, glared at Billy, and shook her head at him. Billy lowered his eyes.

"Rats!" Billy thought to himself. "I got caught! I will have to think of something else to get her attention." Of course, Billy really didn't want to say anything to Sophie; he just wanted to make a disturbance. He did not care anything at all about listening to some old man talk. He would rather have stayed home but it was either go to the library or stay at home with his mom. And staying home was not a good idea. Not today. His mom was having one of her "headaches" which meant she had had too much to drink last night.

Sam observed what Billy had done. He was always doing something to interrupt classes at school and now he was trying to interrupt Mr. Teddy as he spoke. Sam had heard students refer to Billy as "Billy the Bully." Sam didn't like to call people names because it was mean…but "Billy the Bully" sure did fit the description for Billy. Especially today. He wished Billy would settle down so he could listen to Mr. Teddy without being distracted.

~~~

Billy let his mind drift as Mr. Teddy talked. Things didn't used to be so bad at home. Not when his dad was living. He and his dad played catch most days after school and work. Billy loved playing baseball. His dad had played baseball when he was in high school and Billy wanted to play, too.

Since his dad was killed in a car accident last year, his mom just didn't care about him anymore. She worked when she didn't have a hangover. He had to stay quiet and in his room when she didn't work. Like today. If he had stayed home he would have had to stay in his room. There wasn't even any food at home. He only came to the library because he knew that Mrs. Potts always had cookies and lemonade as refreshments after the story hour. His mom rarely bought food anymore. She said that she couldn't afford any food. But she could afford her alcohol.

He used to get good grades in school. His dad would help him with his homework after supper. No one helped him now. He could probably do the homework by himself, but what was the point? No one cared.

« CHAPTER 3 »

Sam was all ears as Mr. Sampson began speaking. He didn't want to miss one word of what the older gentleman had to say about his father's participation in World War I. He loved watching all about World War I on the History Channel and the thought of hearing about that war from someone close to it was just almost too much to hope for.

"Good morning boys and girls." My name is Theodore but everyone just calls me Teddy. I am glad to be here in Giles County visiting my granddaughter, Beth, and her family. Beth, and her daughter, my great-granddaughter, Sophie are here with me today."

Everyone mumbled "hello" and sat up straighter in their chairs as all eyes were on the older gentleman.

Mr. Sampson began. "My father, McFerrin Sampson, was just a young lad of 17 years old when he signed up for the Army. His father had wanted him to stay on the farm and work, but Mack wanted to see the world. He was tired of school and he had worked on that farm all his life. He knew there had to be more to life than farming. Now, can anyone tell me when World War I was fought?"

Sam watched to see if anyone else raised their hand. When no one responded, he slowly raised his hand.

"So, young man, what is your name and when do you think WWI was fought?"

"My name is Sam Baxter. WWI was fought from 1914 to 1918."

"Great answer, Sam! You are correct. WWI began on July 28, 1914 and ended on November 11, 1918. How did you know the answer?" asked Mr. Teddy.

Sam replied, "I find history to be intriguing, so I have watched several documentaries about World War I on the History Channel on TV. That channel is actually my favorite channel to watch. "

"He is such a nerd! Who watches the History Channel?" Billy mumbled under his breath. Sam shot a look at Billy to find that he was staring at the floor.

"The History Channel is a great place to learn about the history of America and other countries." Mr. Teddy glanced at Billy. "I enjoy watching the History Channel, too. Of course, at my age, I don't do as many outdoor activities as I used to, so I watch a lot of television.

"My father joined the Army in November of 1917. After his basic training at Camp Gordon, Georgia, Mack was sent to France. He didn't really want to fight in the war, but he did not have a choice when he was sent over there. I remember my father talking about some of his experiences while he was in France. He didn't talk much about the actual battles that he faced. Like most of the men who fought in the War, they didn't want to live through that horror again by telling their stories. In fact, I brought something with me today that I would like to show you."

Mr. Teddy nodded to his granddaughter. Beth handed him something that was wrapped in a long suede black cloth. Mr. Teddy sat with the item in his lap. He

15

looked over the crowd. His eyes locked on Sam's for just a brief moment, then he said, "What I have here made Mack realize that war was real. And it made him homesick for the family farm."

Sam scooted to the edge of his seat and watched as Mr. Teddy began to unroll the black cloth. Light gleamed off the shiny object. He pulled on the object and Sam saw that it was a sword. A real sword. Mr. Teddy picked up the sword and held it up for everyone to see.

"Mack never used this sword. He found it in France as his troop was walking along the road to Soignies, near the village of Casteau. There was a very significant battle fought in that area that involved Captain Charles Hornby of the 4th Royal Irish Dragoon Guards. Captain Hornby and his men were guarding that particular road where Mack found this sword. Hornby and his squadron became the first unit of the British Expeditionary Force to engage the German army in that area."

Mr. Teddy paused for a few moments to drink a sip of water. Sam wanted to start asking questions. Did this sword belong to Captain Hornby? How did Mack find the sword? When was this battle fought? It was hard to sit still while these thoughts swirled through his head.

Mr. Teddy began to speak again. "Mack never knew who the sword belonged to and thought that it may have belonged to a fallen soldier from that first battle in 1914. Of course, there was no real way to determine who the sword belonged to because there was no name or initials on the sword. But he liked to think that it was from an early battle."

Sam raised his hand. In a quiet voice he asked, "Mr. Teddy, may I ask how Mack found the sword? I mean, if he ever told how he found the sword."

"Sam, that is a great question," declared Mr. Teddy. "Mack always told a story of how he was crawling through some underbrush along the tree line close to the village of Casteau. In fact, when he was crawling along, he felt his britches get snagged on something. He thought it was a briar bush but when he reached down to pull his britches from the briars, his hand touched something hard. He looked to see what had him snagged and saw sunlight reflected off an object in the grass. When he pulled at the object, he saw that it was this sword. He looked around to see if anyone saw him and then he tucked the sword in his belt. The sword was a little heavy but he was excited to have something extra for protection. He carried the sword the rest of the time that he was overseas.

"Mack kept this sword as a reminder of how horrible the war was. Did you know that over 16 million people died during World War I? It was considered one of the deadliest conflicts in the history of the human race."

Everyone sat silently as Mr. Teddy stopped talking. No one moved. It was hard to imagine that so many people had died. Mr. Teddy took another sip of water.

Beth stepped up beside her grandfather. She turned to the group and said, "I believe Mr. Teddy is finished talking but you can come up to speak to him for just a few moments before I take him home."

Leon watched Mr. Teddy for a moment and then looked at Sam. "Let's go outside to wait for your mom."

"You go on. I'll be out in a few minutes. I want to talk to Mr. Teddy." Sam replied.

Billy walked by as Sam was talking with Leon. "You are such a suck up," he whispered to Sam as he nudged Sam with his elbow. Billy walked on out the door.

Sam stood and watched while others talked to Mr. Teddy. Finally, he went up to speak with the older gentleman. Sam shook hands with Mr. Teddy and said, "Thank you for coming to talk to us today. I really enjoyed hearing about Mack and his sword. I thought everything you said was interesting."

"I enjoyed talking with your group, Sam. I know that listening about something that happened so long ago isn't very exciting to young people today."

"I know that some people don't enjoy hearing about history but I have always found history to be fascinating. In fact, I kinda get in trouble in class sometimes because I jump in when the teacher is talking. I forget that I am supposed to wait until she asks questions before I start talking. I guess I just want to share what I have learned. It's a good thing my teacher is patient with me," Sam replied with a grin.

Beth came over to help Mr. Teddy out of his chair. They began to walk toward the door when Mr. Teddy stopped and turned around. "Sam, I will be at my granddaughter's house a couple more weeks. I would enjoy talking with you some more if you could find the time to come over. Sophie can tell you how to get to her house if you need directions."

"Thanks, Mr. Teddy. I'll ask my mom if I can come over. I would enjoy talking with you some more, too."

Sam opened the door. "Sam." Mrs. Potts called to him. "Did you enjoy listening to Mr. Teddy today?"

"Yes mam, I did. I'm glad that you asked him to come today to speak to us."

Sam got a cookie from the tray that Mrs. Potts had set on the table outside the door. He also got a small cup of lemonade. Leon was standing near the entrance waiting for him. "Dude, I thought you were going to stay all day. Whassup with you asking him questions? I was afraid that he was going to talk all day and we wouldn't get to hang out."

Sam shrugged his shoulders. "He invited me to come over to Sophie's house to talk some more about World War I. I thought he was very interesting. How many times do you think we will get to talk with someone about that war? Or even World War II?"

"Hey, there's your mom. Let's go."

The boys ran over to the car and got in. Sally pulled out of the parking lot. "Did y'all have a good time at the reading hour today?"

"Sam did." Leon said in a sarcastic voice.

"Did something special happen at story hour?"

"Mom, there was a man who talked about World War I. His daddy was in the war and he found a sword. It was so neat to see a sword that was that old. Mr. Teddy's daddy always thought that it was from one of the first battles of the war! Oh man, what a find. It would be neat to find something like that!" Sam talked so fast that he forgot to pause for breath.

Sally laughed. "Whoo! Slow down and breathe. I know that you must have enjoyed that, especially knowing how much you love history. What kind of sword did he have?"

"I don't know what kind of sword it was but it was so neat. I may see if I can find it on the internet. Mr. Teddy, that's the man who showed it to us, said that it was probably used to kill someone during the war. That makes me sad to think about people killing each other."

Sally watched her young son in the rearview mirror. His compassion for others was evident in the struggle she saw on his face. She knew he was fascinated with history and the two wars, but she also knew he did not like the killing part. His dad had explained to Sam that war was not always fair.

Leon spoke up, "Hey, Sam, you wanna come over to my house and shoot some hoops? We haven't practiced in a long time."

"Oh, that reminds me, Leon, your mom called and said she was going to be a while longer running errands. She suggested that you stay at our house until she's done and she will pick you up later. The two of you can shoot some hoops while I bake some cookies. Now what is your favorite cookie?", Sally asked with a grin.

"Aw, Mrs. B., you know what kind of cookies I like," Leon said with a laugh.

"Well, why don't I make some chocolate chunk cookies while you two play a little basketball? I will call you when the cookies are ready to eat. Will that work?"

"Sounds good to me, Mrs. B. Billy got most of the cookies at the library." Leon looked at Sam. "Whatcha think, Sam? Ready to take some practice shots?"

"Yeah, I'm ready. Hey, mom, you know that chocolate chunk cookies are my favorite, too. Right? You make the best cookies ever!"

Sally laughed. "I know those are your favorite cookies, too, Sam. I was just checking to see if you were listening." Sally pulled into the driveway. "You boys have fun. I'll call for you when the cookies are ready."

Sally got out of the car and went into the house. The boys got out and went over to the basketball goal that Sam's dad had put up several years ago when Sam had asked to play basketball when he was much younger.

« CHAPTER 4 »

The boys went into the garage to get the basketball. "So, do you want to play a game of horse for practice?" Sam asked Leon.

"Sure. Winner gets to get the first cookie when Mrs. B. gets them ready." Leon grabbed the basketball and began to dribble as he went toward the goal. Leon liked to show off his moves as he dribbled the basketball behind his back and around to his other hand. Leon loved to play basketball…and he was good at the game. He was tall, thin and quick on his feet. Players on other teams knew they had met their match when Leon was on the floor.

Leon took his first shot. "All net!" declared Leon. "Let's see you top that, Sam!" He high-fived Sam as he trotted past him and then pitched the ball to Sam.

Sam caught the basketball as Leon tossed it to him. He dribbled a couple of times, paused to get his bearings, dribble a couple more times.

Are ya gonna dribble all day? Just shoot the ball already," Leon declared.

After a couple more bounces, Sam took a shot. "Yep, all net for me, too!" Sam said with a grin.

The boys continued to play round after round. Leon had not missed any shots. Sam was up to "R" having missed several times.

Sam couldn't seem to focus. He kept thinking about Mack and the things he must have seen during the war. At eleven years old he could not imagine fighting in a war. He thought it was noble to be willing to go to war but he didn't know if he could be away from his family that long.

"Boys! Cookies are hot and ready! Come and get them before they cool off," Mrs. Baxter called to them as she stepped out onto the carport.

Leon tossed the ball into the grass. Sam took off running toward the house. He could smell the cookies from the carport. He realized that he was hungry.

As the boys ate their cookies, after Leon got the first cookie because he was winning the game of horse, Leon said to Sam. "I don't think you were trying too hard at playing horse. You don't usually miss when we're playing. What's going on with you?"

"You're right. I kept wondering when I could go talk with Mr. Teddy some more. I don't want to be a pest to him but I sure would like to hear more about Mack's story. I wonder if he will let me hold the sword. Do you want to go over there with me when I go?"

Leon rolled his eyes at Sam. "Naw, I don't think I want to go. I heard enough history today. I mean, why do I want to hear about something that happened over a hundred years ago? Man, I can barely keep up with the daily school news."

"I guess I just like to hear the stories. I think the uniforms are neat. It is interesting that the uniforms haven't really changed that much over the years. Maybe Mr. Teddy will have a picture of Mack in his uniform."

The boys finished their cookies as Anne Webster pulled into the driveway. Sally gave Leon a covered plate of cookies to take home with him. "Mrs. B. you are the best ever!" declared Leon.

Leon hopped in the car and Anne waved to Sally and Sam before backing out of the driveway.

"Mom, thanks for making cookies for us. I know Leon loves cookies but his mom doesn't get to fix them very often because she works and she has to do a lot for her mom."

Sally gave her son a hug and then went back to the house. Sam continued to stand in the driveway for a few more minutes. Maybe he could call Sophie and check on her great-grandfather. He was hoping to get to see Mr. Teddy at least one more time before he had to go home to Kentucky. He picked up the basketball and took it back to the garage.

~ ~ ~

Sam's dad, Will, was tinkering in the garage after work. Sam was sitting on the stool that sat at the end of the workbench. Will enjoyed woodworking and he was making plans to build a bookshelf in Mikayla's room. He wanted something that would grow with Mikayla with shelves for important treasures like her cheerleading trophies and other things that were important to 14 year-old girls.

"Dad, did you ever have a war hero in your family?"

"A war hero? Well, my great-great-grandfather was a captain during the Civil War in the Confederate Army. Would that suffice as a war hero?"

"Did he ever kill anybody?"

Will studied his son thoughtfully. He knew about Sam's trip to the library earlier that day and that Sam had heard a gentleman talk about the sword that his father had found during World War I. Sam loved history...anyone who knew Sam was aware of that. Sometimes Sam would ponder things he had heard until he had to talk about them to clear his mind.

"Son, war is deadly. During the Civil War, and other wars, people were killed. It was brother against brother...the list goes on about families who turned against their neighbors and each other. I'm sure my great-great-grandfather killed someone, but I am also sure that he didn't want to be there. I don't know of too many people who want to be in a war.

"Robert L. Evans was a captain in the Confederate Army, Company 1, 53rd Tennessee Regiment. He's buried in the Lynwood Cemetery. I'll take you there to see his grave someday soon.

"We don't know much about Captain Evans, but I'm sure he was a hero to our family. But know that everyone's perception of a hero is different. While we may think of him as a hero, others may not see him that way. You have to be careful talking about the Civil War so as not to offend anyone."

Sam sat there for a few minutes. He had never heard of this Captain Evans. He wondered if he had had any memorabilia from the Civil War or if he just wanted to forget that it had happened. He knew a lot of people were ashamed to know that they had family that fought during that war.

Mikayla came to the door. "Mom said to tell you that supper is ready."

Will looked up at her as she stood at the door. It was as if he was seeing her for the first time in a while. Mikayla was almost fifteen years old...going on twenty. Her dark, curly hair was waist length and pulled back from her face. Her dark eyes were like coals of fire when she was angry, but they sparkled like stars when she was happy.

She, like Sam, was generous and thoughtful. She enjoyed helping people in her own way, but as a teenager, she loved being on her phone, too. But, she was like Sam in that she got good grades in school.

Will sighed. He was afraid to think what would happen to his heart when she started dating seriously. After all, she was daddy's girl.

She stepped into the shop and saw a drawing laying on the workbench. "Dad, is this a picture of what my bookshelves are going to look like?"

"Well, it's a start. I thought you could look at it and let me know what you think. If you have any ideas on what you want, then you need to let me know so I can make them to suit your needs. After all, these are your bookshelves.," Will said with a laugh.

"Well, I like what I see now but I will look at this and see if I want to make any changes. Do you think we could put lights around the inside of the middle section? The lights would help when I am studying, or when I put on my makeup." She flashed Will a mischievous grin.

"I'm all for the studying part but I think you are beautiful with or without makeup." Will hugged her close for a moment. He could not believe that Mikayla and Sam were growing up so fast. He and Sally just brought them home from the hospital a few days ago…or so it seemed. He sighed. While they were growing older, so was he.

~ ~ ~

They went into the den where Sally had the phone to her ear. "Yes, Sophie, I will let Sam know. Tomorrow at two o'clock. I know he will be excited about seeing Mr. Teddy again. Thank you for calling." Sally hung up the phone.

"Am I going to see Mr. Teddy tomorrow?" Sam asked.

"Yes. That was Sophie on the phone and she told me that Mr. Teddy wanted to see you again. He said he knew that you were very interested in talking about the war. Do you want to check with Leon to see if he wants to go, too?"

"I don't think Leon is too interested in hearing more about the war. I'll tell him about it when I see him in a few days. He wants me to do a sleepover at his house so we can practice hoops."

"That sounds good to me. Now let's eat supper while it's still hot," Sally replied.

~ ~ ~

After supper Sam went to his room. The nerf basketball was still laying on the dresser. The soldier that he had knocked off the dresser that morning was still on the floor. He really should pick that up and put it away, but he didn't. He examined the walls of his room. He had pictures of some of his basketball heroes pinned up on the walls. He also had some football posters on his wall. Dad had put a shelf on his wall and he put some army figurines on the shelf. There were a couple of trophies he had gotten over the years where he had played football and basketball. Then he remembered the sword that Mr. Teddy showed the group that morning at the library. Wouldn't it be neat to have a sword hanging above the shelf? That would be a great addition to his room.

He laid across his bed. He began to go over all that Mr. Teddy had told them about Mack and how he wanted to see the world but not during a war. What would happen if he had to fight in a war? Dad had said that war was not easy no matter what the circumstances were.

He wondered what he and Mr. Teddy would talk about tomorrow. He was excited that he was going to see him again. Billy called him a nerd because he liked history, but Sam was really looking forward to talking with someone who had a love for history like he did. He rolled over on his bed. It was time to sleep but he knew that sleep would be a long time coming tonight. His mind was full of questions about World War I.

Maybe he should do a little more research online before we went to see Mr. Teddy tomorrow. He could do that first thing in the morning right after breakfast. Yeah, that's what he would do.

« CHAPTER 5 »

Leon and his mom were on their way to the grocery store. His Grandma June was not feeling well and they had to get groceries and medicine for her. It seemed as though they were always running errands for her. Leon didn't really mind helping his grandmother. He loved her and she had always been good to him, but he had really wanted to stay with Sam a little longer so they could practice hoops. Of course, Sam wasn't in the mood to practice. His mind was completely on the stories that Mr. Teddy told them at the library.

Sam was Leon's best friend. They had been friends since they were four years old. He had loved living next door to Sam. Mrs. B., Sam's mother, was always so nice to him and let him spend a lot of time at their house. His mom and dad had fought a lot during those years and when he was at Sam's house he didn't have to listen to them argue. He and his brother, Jarius, looked for any excuse to be away from home.

If Leon wasn't at Sam's house, he was at Grandma June's. She didn't like the way his mom and dad argued in front of him and Jarius, so she would let them stay with her most weekends. His grandfather, Pops, had died a couple months ago, but Pops loved the game of basketball. In his youth, Pops was tall and thin, and was a star basketball player in high school and later, college. Pops could have gone professional, but he and Grandma June had married during their college years and, well, they began to have children so Pops felt that he needed to get a 'real' job, as he called it, and settle down to a family life. He told Leon and Jarius that he never regretted being at home with his Junie and the children.

But Pops never lost his zeal for basketball. He coached basketball for Saturday league for years. "Just because you don't play the game anymore doesn't mean you can't teach others to play," he often told Leon. So, for nearly fifty years he did just that. Everyone called his grandpa "Pops" or "Coach." Leon could remember being on the basketball court when he was only two years old because Pops took him and Jarius to every practice and game.

Pops took him to a Harlem Globetrotters game before he died. Leon told his Pops, "I want to learn to dribble like those men. I want to shoot the ball over my head, through my legs, and jump over a player if I have to, to make the score. Can you teach me how to play like that, Pops?"

Pops looked at him for several seconds with a sad look to his face. Finally he said, "I have taught you how to play the game and I will help you to do some fancy footwork, but you are going to have to practice a lot if you want to play like these men."

Pops pulled Leon close to his chest and said, "I will always be proud of you, Son. Never forget that. All I ask is that you always give the game your best. The other moves will come as you practice. But remember this: always be a gentleman on the floor. Never show bad sportsmanship. When your team loses, man up and be the first to shake hands with the winner. And when you make a goal, act like you've been there before. Don't go whooping and a hollering and hanging off the goal. Be ready for the next play, because while you're celebrating, the other team is planning their next play. Keep your head in the game and you will always be a step ahead of the other team. I can't give you any better advice than that."

Leon didn't realize that Pops was so sick. He knew that his grandfather coughed a lot, but Pops always said it "was just a cold. Nothing to worry about, Son." But it *was* something to worry about. Pops had finally gone to the doctor. He was told that he had lung cancer. Pops died within a few months of being diagnosed. But that didn't keep him from the basketball games.

Leon was in sixth grade. Pops died just after basketball season ended. He could still hear Pops tell him, "Keep your mind in the game, Son, and you will overcome your opponent every time. Don't ever let the other team see you get rattled. Once you lose your confidence in yourself or your team, well, the game is lost."

Pops always had a positive thing to say, even if they lost a game. "Son, when you play your best, it doesn't matter whether you win or lose. It's how you feel about yourself when the game is over. When you play your best game you can walk off the floor a winner, even if the scoreboard says differently. If you know that you didn't play your best and you lose the game, then you have to kick off the dust, practice harder, and give it your best the next time you play. The best thing you can do is never give up."

Leon thought about his Pops every time he picked up a basketball. He tried to practice every day, but it wasn't always easy. He was fortunate because he had a basketball goal at home and at Grandma June's. Pops saw to that. He installed both of them so that he would know that both goals were set to regulations.

Leon remembered that when he was four, Pops had installed the goal at his house. Leon tried so hard to get that basketball up to the net, but he could not make it. One day, after practicing for about fifteen minutes, his mother came out and said, "Pops, you need to lower that goal. You know that boy can't get that ball up there. It's too high for him."

"How is he ever going to learn to make a goal if I lower it and make it easy for him? He needs to man up and learn to jump to make the shot."

"Pops, he is four years old. Give him a chance to hit the goal. As he grows and gains confidence in himself, then you can raise the goal. I don't think you're being fair to him."

Leon remembered that Pops just stood there staring at his daughter. "Annie, did I not teach you to play the game? Did I mollycoddle you? No siree! I taught you to jump and get the ball up there. If you can do it, so can he."

Annie stood there for a minute. With her hands on her hips, she said, "You know that I was nearly six years old before I started practicing. You wouldn't let me play because you thought I was too frail. I had been sickly when I was smaller and you were afraid that I wasn't physically strong enough. Also, if you remember, I did a lot of my practicing on a real court and the goals were lower for the smaller kids. Now, lower that goal and give my boy a chance to learn how to play the game. You can raise it when he is taller." She stood and stared at Pops with 'the look' that Moms have.

Leon almost laughed out loud at that memory. He remembered how Pops grumbled about how "A boy can't learn if he is mollycoddled. I ain't about to raise a sissy. That Annie knows better than to question me. I've been coaching kids longer than she has been alive."

All the while that Pops was muttering to himself, he had gotten his tools out of his truck and lowered the goal. Leon recalled his excitement when he threw the ball up and made a score. He and Pops jumped up and down and whooped and hollered as if they were at a real ballgame. Yeah, his Pops was the best…and now he really missed him.

Leon stood looking at the goal, his memories of Pops washing over him. His mom was helping Grandma June take the medicine they had gotten her earlier. He sure hoped that his grandma was going to be okay. He didn't think that he could lose her, too. He heard a basketball bounce on the driveway.

Pops! He turned to look and there stood his mom.

"You know," she paused, "Pops taught me how to play the game, too. Now I may not be able to coach as well as he did, but I can help you practice."

Leon watched as his mom continued to dribble the ball. She hunched over and while never taking her eyes off of him, she began moving around him and before he could react, she made a run for the goal and layed up one of the most beautiful hook shots he had ever seen. He had never even seen Pops make that kinda shot, and Pops could hit the goal from anywhere on the court!

Annie laughed as she saw Leon's expression. "What! Did you think I was a sissy? Pops never made it easy for me. In fact, I was always told that I had an unfair advantage because Coach was my dad. What no one realized was that because my dad *was* Coach, I had to work harder than everyone else because he wasn't about to play favorites...even if I was his only child. I had to learn to play better than the boys if I wanted to be in the game. And he had me practice with the boys more than I practiced with the girls."

"You practiced with the boys? I have never heard of a girl practicing with the boys. The coaches at school have the boys and girls practice at different times so that we aren't distracted by trying to watch each other."

"I was allowed to practice with the boys because he coached the Saturday league. When his team practiced during the week, he had me practice with them. He thought that it would toughen me up and give me more stamina. He was right about that. At first the boys didn't want to guard me because I was a girl and they were afraid that I would get hurt. But after I made a few hook shots and three pointers, well, that seemed to rile them up so they began treating me like one of them. They never made it easy for me after that."

"Mom, why haven't you ever told me that you could play? I mean, I know that you have always supported me and been at most of my games, but I thought you did that because, well, you're my mom and you're supposed to support me."

"Leon, Pops was the best coach in the county. He loved basketball more than anything in this world. Well, except for Grandma June, me, and you and your brother. He wanted to be the one to teach you to play the game. He was so proud of you and Jarius. The two of you gave him extended life because, through you, he could still play the game.

Before Pops died, he made me promise that I would make time to practice with you. I have to admit that before today I just couldn't do it. The thought of picking up a basketball without Pops being around was more than I could take. I miss him more than I ever thought possible. I have realized that if I want to see you progress in the game, and if I want to keep Pops' memory alive, then I need to help you practice."

Annie looked at Leon as if she needed to tell him something. Then with a quirky smile, she said, "Well, I had planned to tell you this later, after we got home, but I have been asked to coach the Saturday league. I won't do it if you think that you will be too embarrassed to have your momma out there coaching the boys. I think I could do a good job but I will need you to help me. You know the rules and regs better than anyone. I know, because Pops taught them to you all your life. What do you think? Can you and I be a team?"

Leon stood looking at him mom, then he ran over to her and threw his arms around her. "Mom, I think that's great! We will make a great team. Pops would be very proud if you carried on his legacy. I would never be embarrassed to have you teach me and the team. Can I tell Sam that you're going to be our coach?"

Annie hugged her son tightly to her. She had tears in her eyes at her son's maturity and understanding. She laughed, "You can tell whomever you want to, but by all means, you can tell Sam."

Leon unwrapped his arms from around his mother and ran toward the house. Just as he neared the steps, he stopped, turned and said, "And all this time I thought you were a real sissy!" He laughed out loud when his mother threw the basketball at him...and missed.

CHAPTER 6

Sam woke up. He was laying on top of the covers. He had a blanket spread over him. Mom must have come in during the night and covered him up. The last thing he remembered was thinking about his trip today to see Mr. Teddy. At that thought, he jumped up from bed and took off for breakfast. It was going to be a great day!

"Whoa! Slow down there. What is your rush this morning?" Sally asked her son.

"I'm going to see Mr. Teddy today and I want to do some research on the internet before we go. I told him that I love history and especially World War I and II history. What if he asks me some questions and I don't know the answer. I don't want to look dumb."

"First of all I don't think Mr. Teddy is going to give you a quiz today. He just wants to visit with you. I have no idea what you will be discussing but don't go stressing out about it. Just relax and enjoy the conversation."

Sam rolled his eyes and sighed. "You're right. I could hardly sleep last night for thinking about today. I will do some research but I don't want to appear that I have all the answers. I guess I'm just excited." Sam stood up from the breakfast table and went toward the den and the computer. When he got to the doorway he turned and went to his mom. He hugged her and said, "By the way, thanks for covering me up with the blanket last night. I guess I fell asleep before I got in the bed."

Annie hugged her son a little tighter. She realized that he would soon be at the age when he would not be so quick to hug her. "You're welcome. I knew that you were worn out from all the excitement of going to see Mr. Teddy again. I didn't want to wake you so I just covered you up. Now go get cleaned up and then do your research."

~~~

Sally was driving Sam to see Mr. Teddy the next afternoon. He had talked about the trip all morning. "Sam, I know how excited you get when you start talking about history, but please remember that Mr. Teddy is older and he will tire easily.

When you notice that he is getting tired, text me and I will come pick you up. Also remember to talk slowly, clearly and a little loud so Mr. Teddy can understand what you're saying. I know that when you get excited you forget to slow down when you're talking. Okay?"

"Okay, Mom. I will try to remember. I can't imagine what Mr. Teddy wants to talk about today. Do you think he has any other memorabilia from the war?"

"I don't know if he has anymore or not but let him control the conversation. Don't ask too many questions. I know how respectful you are to elderly people but, as your Mom, I just need to remind you how to behave."

Sam rolled his eyes at his mom, and then wiggled his eyebrows. "Thanks for the reminder. I know I can get

pretty hyper when I'm excited. I'll try to control myself."
Sam laughed out loud. So did Sally.

~~~

"Come in, Sam. I've been waiting for you. How are you today? Did you have a hard time finding our house?"

"Hello, Mr. Teddy. No, sir. My mom knew the way. Thank you for inviting to visit with you today. I really enjoyed hearing about Mack yesterday at the library. I have been thinking a lot about some of the things you shared with us."

"Well, I thought we could talk some more about World War I. So, what interests you about that war?"

"I'm really intrigued about the Christmas Truce of 1914. I am amazed at how a war was stopped for a day."

Mr. Teddy looked thoughtful for a moment. "I was always fascinated with that Truce as well. You can't help but wonder that if they could stop a war for a day, then why couldn't the war be stopped altogether. Or not even started at all. But that's another topic of discussion that we don't want to get into today. We can't solve all the mysteries of war in one day, can we?.

"I have done some research about the Christmas Truce of 1914. Did you know that this Christmas Truce was the last official Christmas Truce during a war? I thought that was interesting."

"I think I had heard that." Sam replied but he realized that Mr. Teddy wasn't really asking for a response from him. He was merely stating a fact.

40

Mr. Teddy continued. "There were certain periods of 'quiet time' before the Christmas Truce when the soldiers agreed not to shoot at each other. Between battles and out of boredom, soldiers began to banter, even barter for cigarettes, between opposite sides. Informal truces were also agreed and used as an opportunity to recover wounded soldiers, bury the dead and shore up damaged trenches. Many of the soldiers felt that these short truces were a part of the etiquette of war.

"By early December 1914, the soldiers realized that the war would not be over by Christmas. Most of them were homesick and wanted the war to be over so they could go home. In fact, Pope Benedict XV had proposed an official 'Truce of God' where all hostilities would cease over the Christmas period, but the authorities rejected that idea. However, they did want to maintain morale and bring some festive cheer to those on the front. So, it was only a small portion of soldiers that celebrated the Christmas Truce, but those who did, remembered it for a long time. Many soldiers sent letters home describing the truce and how it affected them for many days afterward.

"A short time before Mack joined the army, the United States entered the war. The U.S. had desperately tried to stay neutral, but ties to Britain, propaganda, the sinking of ships by German U-boats and a German attempt to get Mexico to declare war on the U.S. pushed the U.S. into getting involved. The United States declared war on April 6, 1917.

"I'm sure Mack never thought that he would actually go to France. He probably thought he would stay state-side and travel to other stares. But the army was sending a lot of the young men over there after their basic training. Mack wanted to see more of the world but I don't think fighting in a war was how he intended to do that," Mr. Teddy said with a chuckle.

"Did I mention Mack's good buddy, Henry Puryear? They actually met at Camp Gordon. Even though both of them were from Giles County, they had never met before basic training. Henry and Mack were sent overseas to fight and thankfully, both of them returned from the war.

They were in the field artillery unit where they saw a lot of action. Mack was actually wounded during a battle and Henry carried him to safety. Mack always believed that Henry saved his life. When they came home after the war, Henry moved away but they stayed in touch through the years until Mack died."

Mr. Teddy sat for a few minutes. Sam wondered if he should text his mom to come get him. While trying to decide what to do, Mr. Teddy looked at him and said, "Sam, things are not always fair in war. A lot of innocent people were killed. Although Adolph Hitler volunteered to fight during WWI, he became a bitter man who blamed the Jews for the anti-war sentiment among German civilians. He saw them as conspiring to spread unrest and undermine the German war effort. During WWII he took his hatred of Jews to a new level, having many of them killed.

"A lot of our men and women from America were killed after we joined the WWII effort. But I won't bore you with more history. You can look up all that I have told you on the internet. We had a lot of brave men and women who fought in those two wars and many wars since then. We continue to have many men and women who are heroes. Heroes aren't always people who fight in wars...they are average people who do for their neighbors.

"Keep studying history because you can learn so much about our great country by doing so. Unfortunately there is a lot of unrest in our country today. In the Bible the Gospel of Mark 3:25 states: 'And if a house is divided against itself, that house cannot stand.' Abraham Lincoln used this quote in a speech he gave in 1858 before he was elected president. Our country needs to rally together if we are to remain strong."

Mr. Teddy paused, then said, "Thank you for spending your time with an old man. You have made my visit more enjoyable. Remember, Sam, to always be kind to others, especially those who are less fortunate than you. Maybe we will see each other again before I go home."

Mr. Teddy closed his eyes. Sam continued to sit there quietly. Sophie came in the room and motioned for Sam to follow her. He looked over at Mr. Teddy who still had his eyes closed. He tiptoed from the room and into the foyer.

"Sam, thank you for visiting my Grandfather Teddy. I cannot tell you how much he enjoyed spending time with you and talking about his dad. You have a great gift for listening."

Sophie opened the door. "Will you be at the library tomorrow? My mom is going to take me for the story hour. I hope you will be there, too."

"I will ask my mom if I can go. I'm not sure what her plans are but I will try. Please tell Mr. Teddy that I really enjoyed meeting him and hearing him talk about his dad. It was cool to hear the stories. He has given me a lot to think about. I will be looking up some more facts on the internet. I never thought that I would be able to talk with Mr. Teddy again. He is a great man. It was an honor to meet and talk with him. I enjoyed listening to him."

~ ~ ~

Sam was greeted by Mrs. Potts when he walked into the library the next day. "Sam, I understand that you spent some more time with Mr. Teddy yesterday. Did you enjoy your visit?"

Sam was surprised that Mrs. Potts knew about his visit with Mr. Teddy but he answered, "Yes mam. I did enjoy my time with him. It is amazing what Mr. Teddy knows. I wish I knew that much about history."

Mrs. Potts laughed, "Well now, Mr. Teddy has lived a few more years than you but I believe that when you are Mr. Teddy's age you will know as much, if not more, than

Mr. Teddy. You just keep your passion for history and keep doing research and learning.

"Now go on into the reading room. I think we have a project that you will enjoy getting involved in. There are several others already in the room. I'll be there in a few minutes." She began to move her hands as if looking for something. She patted the top of her head, then remembered the chain around her neck. She put on her glasses and headed toward the librarian's desk. Sam almost burst out laughing. Mrs. Potts was a very nice woman, a little spacey, but nice.

Sam went into the reading room. Sophie, Leon, Billy and several others were already sitting in the chairs.

Billy saw Sam and said, "Well, I guess we are having another history lesson today because 'Mr. History' is here." Billy just laughed as Sam turned red. Sam sat down in a chair next to Leon.

Mrs. Potts came into the room with Beth, Sophie's mother. "Boys and girls we have a great surprise for you. Sophie's mother is a play director. She has seen your interest in the things that Mr. Teddy has been sharing about World War I and she would like to do a summer play about some of the things he has shared. She would like for all of you to be in the play. How does that sound to you?"

Sam thought it would be interesting but he didn't know about being in a play. Basketball camp would be starting soon and he needed to concentrate on the game. He wasn't sure he had time to learn lines to be in a play.

~~~

"Hey, Sam! Wait up!" Leon yelled as he ran out the door of the library. Where was Sam going in such a hurry? Had he forgotten that they were supposed to practice some hoops at his house this afternoon? "Sam!"

Sam turned when he heard Leon shouting his name. "Oh, hey, Leon. I forgot that I'm going to your house. I guess I'm just surprised about the library doing a play. Are you going to be in the play?"

"I will if you will. I think it might be kinda fun to dress up in uniforms and carry swords. I thought you liked swords."

"I do like swords but what about basketball camp? How will we have time to learn lines and practice basketball? I don't see how we can do both."

"Well, maybe we won't have to learn lines."

Sam looked at Leon. "What do you mean 'maybe we won't have to learn lines'? How can we be in a play and not have to learn lines?"

Leon laughed out loud and elbowed him in the ribs. "We can ask for walk-on parts. You know, be in the background. We can be soldiers that carry swords but don't say anything." Leon leaned in closer to Sam to whisper: "Sophie is going to be in the play."

Sam glared at Leon. "What's that supposed to mean?"

"Nothing! I was just kidding, man! I still think we oughta be in the play. It could be a lot of fun. Maybe we ought to practice our sword skills instead of shooting hoops this afternoon." Leon thrust his arm out as though he had a sword in his hand.

Sam jumped back, surprised at Leon's quick motion. "Let me think about it, Leon. I need to talk to my mom and dad about this. It could be interesting. Now let's get over to your house so we can practice hoops."

Billy walked up to Sam and Leon. "Ooh, are we going to dress up like little soldiers and wave our swords in the air?" Billy asked as he swung his arms wildly, as though he had a sword in his hands. Then in a high-pitched voice he whined, "Oh, kind sir, please do not stick your sword in me. I am just a poor, simple boy with no money and no food." Billy doubled over with laughter.

Sam looked at Billy with a scowl on his face. "Billy, war isn't anything to make fun of. You heard Mr. Teddy say that a lot of people were killed in the war."

"Aw come on! Everybody likes to play soldier and you do, too, so just admit it. I bet you have a whole bunch of toy soldiers in your toy chest." Billy straightened his shoulders and held out his arm as though he was holding a sword. He turned and looked at Sam. Then he clicked his heels together and saluted Sam. "Heil Hitler!"

Sam stared at Billy. How could he be such a moron? Billy was always trying to cause trouble.

"Mom's here, Sam. Let's go," Leon said as he pulled Sam away from Billy.

"Have fun with your little toy soldiers!" Billy called after them as they walked away.

Sam could hear Billy laughing as they got into Anne Webster's car. Why did Billy have to act so weird sometimes? He wanted to be nice to Billy but it was hard when he acted like such a doofus. Sam kept these thoughts to himself. He knew that Leon had a hard time with Billy, too.

Sam thought about the play on the way over to Leon's house. It did sound as though it would be fun and maybe they could get non-speaking parts. Leon sure was goofy. He just didn't figure Leon to be so excited about a play, especially one about history.

And what was that remark about Sophie being in the play? He barely knew her! He had seen her at school but they had different classes and he didn't see her very much. His mom had told him that Sophie was going to be a cheerleader for the basketball team this year so they would probably see each other more often since he was on the basketball team. And they would both be in the play this summer.

CHAPTER 7

Play practice had begun. Sam and Leon did get walk-on parts so they did not have to learn lines but they did have to learn their cues so that they would know when to go out on the stage. Sam had also volunteered to help with some of the sound checks and background props when he wasn't needed on the stage.

The whole family had gotten involved. Will had been building backdrops in his shop the past week. He had already cut out and painted trees for the forest.

Beth, Mr. Teddy's granddaughter, also wanted a castle painted on a painter's drop cloth that could be hung from the ceiling. Will and Beth had finally decided on the design of the castle and he would work on that this week.

Will was enjoying getting to do some woodworking and painting. He had been too busy at work for a few months and had not been able to do much in his shop. His shop was his haven away from everything else.

Sally was helping with costumes. She loved to do crafting and sewing. Most of the costumes could be ordered for the soldiers as well as some of the outfits for the girls.

Sally had been making accessories that would make the costumes look more authentic. She had been busy on the phone asking friends to look through old trunks to find articles from the time period of WWI that could be used as props. She had also looked at thrift stores and consignment shops. She had found some great accessories that could be used. Some of the items she found were reproductions, but they would work well. She had done a lot of research online so that she could match what accessories were needed with each costume.

Mikayla also had a part in the play. She had the role of Princess Mary. She loved the part of dressing up as a princess. She had been reading about Princess Mary and had not realized that she worked as a nurse during WWI. While she only worked two days a week, she knew that she was doing her part for the War effort. The Princess had a full life as she was involved in many worthwhile causes during her lifetime.

Mikayla had been walking around with a costume tiara on her head. She practiced walking with her head held erect. She was also practicing her knighting skills. She had even named Will, Sir William and had begun calling him that around the house. Will wasn't always amused at his new title, especially when she would say "Sir William, I need you to take me to the mall so I can shop for new clothes." Yeah, his princess needed to join the ranks of the lowly people again. Royalty had gone to her head.

Sophie played a nurse for the hospital scene that included a wounded soldier and Princess Mary. She took her role seriously and studied hard to know her lines. She had even done some research online on how to wrap bandages. She wanted to be the best nurse possible. This could be a vocation for her as she might decide to become a nurse in real life. Saving lives seemed to be a worthwhile profession to her.

Leon was one of the stage managers. He helped cue the others as to when to be onstage in between the times that he was to be on stage. He told Sam that if he didn't get a basketball scholarship and an offer to play professional basketball that he might become a play director. He enjoyed getting to 'boss' the others about when and where to be throughout the play. Leon was a good leader on and off the basketball court.

Billy had a walk-on part as one of the soldiers. He constantly annoyed everyone while he tried to stab them with the fake swords. Leon told him to calm down many times during a rehearsal. Billy never saw the need to take the whole play seriously as he was "just having fun." The rehearsals were a good way to get away from home during the day otherwise he would have been stuck at home most of the time. There were usually snacks backstage for everyone to enjoy. Billy didn't always have food at home so snacks were good. Beth and Sophie provided transportation for Billy to and from rehearsal. He was always respectful and thanked Beth for picking him up and taking him home. Billy knew how to use his manners; he just chose not to use them most of the time.

The play was in two weeks and everyone had worked hard to learn their lines. A dress rehearsal was planned for Saturday afternoon. Beth thought that if they had an early dress rehearsal that it would allow time to make any adjustments that were needed before the real performance began. Everyone had worked overtime to get backdrops, sceneries, and costumes ready.

Beth was pleased with the progress of the play. All the students and their parents had worked diligently to make this play enjoyable for everyone to see. The proceeds from the play were to be used toward the library for new software and supplies; and a plaque in honor of Mr. Teddy.

Mr. Teddy had extended his stay with Beth and Sophie. He was very excited to be the source when scenes needed to be verified. After all, Mr. Teddy had studied about WWI and was considered an expert on that era.

~ ~ ~

Beth stood on the stage. She had a brass box in her hands. She called everyone to sit down for a few minutes. "I want to thank everyone for your hard work these past few weeks. The painted scenes are realistic. Whenever I see the backdrops, I feel as though I have been transported back in time. The costumes and accessories are authentic looking. I know that it has taken many, many hours for these projects. I am amazed at all that has been done in such a short time. All of you parents have been so patient with me and my requests. I have directed many plays and have worked with many volunteers, but I have to say that all of you have outperformed all other projects that I have participated in. The students have done an excellent job at learning their lines and being prompt and respectful. I realize that we have pulled off a huge feat in getting this play performance ready in such a short time. All of you are to be commended for your hard work."

Leon poked Sam in the ribs. "She hasn't seen some of the stunts Billy has pulled during these practices. I don't care if he is 'Billy the Bully' because the next time I have to tell him to stop jabbing somebody with his sword, I am going to take him down myself. He has been nothing but a real pain. I don't know why she let him be in the play." Leon just shook his head in frustration.

"You do realize that Billy is twice your size, don't you? Besides, this is almost over. You can endure him for a few more practices and then the play for two nights."

Leon groaned. He had forgotten that they were going to do the performance for two nights. It was going to be a long two weeks...and two nights!

"I want to share some history with you before we begin our dress rehearsal," Beth was saying to the group. "This brass box that I am holding is a true find. You see, it is one of the original brass boxes that Princess Mary sent to the troops during World War I. She understood that many of the soldiers were homesick and she wanted to give them something to boost their morale during Christmas.

"We will not be using this box during the play because it is so old and we don't want it to be harmed, so we have a replica that we will be using. I just wanted all of you to see what the real box looked like. I wanted to thank my grandfather, Mr. Teddy, for finding this for me. He found it through the internet. I am very proud of him for learning how to maneuver the internet. It wasn't easy for him at his age, but Sophie and I kept working with him until he was comfortable with the computer. It has helped him with his research since he can't get out as much now. He won't be here for the dress rehearsals but he will be here for the performances."

Everyone crowded around Beth to look at the beautiful box. There were many oohs and aahs but no one tried to touch the antique brass box.

"Sam, please take this box into the back and put it on the shelf for me. Then give the fake box to Leon so he can keep it close by to use during rehearsal. Now, everyone, take your places. It's time to begin practice." Beth declared as she stepped off the stage.

Sam and Leon went into the back room to put up the beautiful brass box. Sam looked at Leon, "I didn't expect it to be so fancy. I thought it was just a plain box but it has some etching on it. Look at this. It has "Christmas 1914", and the names of some countries who were probably allies with Britain, and a likeness of Princess Mary. How cool is that?"

Leon looked at the box more closely. "I didn't realize that was Princess Mary's image but I couldn't see it very well out there. You're right, this is cool."

The boys saw the shelf where Beth had said to put the box. Sam reached up to the shelf and realized that he needed something to stand on because the shelf was too high for him to reach. He saw a chair over in the corner.

"Hey Leon, bring that chair over here so I can reach the shelf. Okay?"

"Sure, I'll get it." Leon brought the chair over. It was a little wobbly but Sam thought if Leon held onto it then it would be okay.

Sam stood up on the chair. He still couldn't reach the shelf. The chair had arms on it so he stood on the arms and even had to stand on his tiptoes to reach the shelf, but even at that he could barely reach it. Just as he almost had the box on the shelf, Billy yelled "Watch out!"

Sam jerked his head to the right to see what Billy was yelling about. He lost his footing with the brass box still in his hand. Leon tried to hold the chair but he could not get a good grip on it. Sam felt himself falling. Then there was a big flash of light and Sam fell into darkness.

« CHAPTER 8 »

December 1914

Sam could hear Leon hollering at him. It sounded as though Leon was in a barrel. Sam wondered why Leon was yelling at him when they were supposed to be quiet in the theater. Sam raised his head. Sweat streamed down Leon's dark face. "Leon, what's wrong with you?" Sam asked in a voice that sounded far away.

Leon's eyes widened as he said, "Sam, I don't know what just happened but we are not in the theater anymore. Look around you. I don't know where we are! And it's cold."

Sam sat up and looked around. Nothing looked familiar to him. Leon was right. They appeared to be in a forest. The underbrush was wet and cold. He heard a moaning sound close by. "Leon!" Sam whispered. "What is that moaning noise? Is there something in the bushes?"

Leon looked toward the bushes. He stood up to go toward them when he saw Billy stand up. "What's going on here?" Billy bellowed. "What have y'all done to me? And where are we?"

Sam could hear shouting in the distance and he felt a pounding on the ground. He caught a movement to his left which made him look toward the trees. A young boy stood in the shadows of a tall tree. Then the boy motioned for them to come to him. Sam didn't know what to do. Who was the boy and where were they?

"Leon, that boy is beckoning us to come to him. Do you know who he is?"

Leon looked toward the trees. He looked at Sam and whispered, "I don't have any idea who he is but I think we need to go over to the trees with him. It feels like a herd of horses is running towards us. Can you walk?"

Sam stood up with Leon's help. He felt okay. He shook his legs one at a time. Yep, his legs felt okay, too. He looked at Billy and said, "Come on, Billy! We can't just stand here." Billy shuddered as though he had been asleep, and then he began to run with them towards the boy in the trees. Just as they reached the trees a loud noise sounded behind them.

A group of men in funny looking costumes rode over the spot where they had just left. Dust from the horses' hooves rose above the ground. Leon sneezed. Loudly. Sam put his hand over Leon's mouth and said, "Be quiet! Do you want them to hear us?"

Leon just looked at Sam. His eyes grew large over Sam's hand. Then Leon reached up and pushed Sam's hand off his face. "I can't help it if the dust made me sneeze! We need to figure out what is going on around here."

Leon turned his head to the little boy. "Who are you?" he asked, "and WHERE are we?"

The three boys were looking at the young lad. The little boy had on loose britches that looked too big for him. His shirt hung on his small frame with sleeves that reached below his fingertips. His hair was not blonde but not dark

57

brown either. His eyes were neither blue nor green. He looked as though he was as scared of them as they were of him. They thought that he might take off running.

The little boy said something that sounded as though he was speaking in a foreign language. Then he pointed to his chest and said, "Henri."

Sam pointed to himself and said "Sam." He motioned toward Leon and said "Leon." Then he pointed at Billy and said "Billy." The little boy stood looking at them. Sam asked, "Do you speak English? Where are we?"

Henri answered. "Yes, I speak a little English. You are in the village of Casteau."

Leon looked at Sam and Billy. Then he looked at Henri. "Where the heck is Casteau? Are we near the park? And who were those men that just rode by on horses? I mean, well, I don't know what I mean." Leon threw up his hands as if he was surrendering himself to defeat

"Casteau is in Belgium and is a village near the French and German borders. How can you not know where you are? Don't you know where you live?"

Sam and Leon sank to the ground. "Belgium? France? How did we get here, Sam?" questioned Leon.

"What the heck are y'all talking about? We were just in the theater and now we are in the woods! Somebody has some explaining to do here," Billy said with a growl.

"Billy! Keep your voice down. Do you want those men to hear us and come back? Until we know where we are we need to keep our voices down," Sam retorted.

"Those looked like German soldiers that were riding on the horses. Henri, what is the date today?" Sam asked.

Henri just stared at him. "The date? You don't know what day it is? Did you hit your head when you fell?"

Sam looked intently at Henri for a moment. He noticed that Henri's clothes, even though they were too large for him, they seemed to be from a different time period. He remembered seeing a young boy on the History Channel wearing similar clothes but he could not remember which show he was watching at the time. His thoughts swirled in his brain and he almost felt dizzy.

"It is December, 1914. Today is the 22nd. Christmas is almost here."

"Leon, something tells me we are not in Elkton anymore. Somehow we have gone back in time to World War I. Mr. Teddy was just talking about his father, Mack, being in World War I and now we are here. I don't know how this could happen. Do you? I must be watching too much television." Sam put his hand to his brow.

"Have you lost your mind? How can it be 1914?" Billy declared. "We must be in the woods in the back of the library. Where did you get your costume?" He asked Henri. "It doesn't look like the ones we are using for the play. And I don't remember seeing you during practice, either."

Sam whirled and looked hard at Billy. "Billy! We are *not* behind the library. Somehow we have gone back in time. Did you see a flash when I fell off the chair? That must have been when we were sent to this time."

"That's impossible! Time travel isn't real. It's just science fiction." Billy whispered with a tremble in his voice.

Leon shook his head. "I don't even like history and now you're telling me that we have traveled back in time during World War I? This is crazy!"

The three boys just looked at each other. "Surely this was all a dream," Sam thought." Maybe I hit my head when I fell and I'm dreaming all of this." He sure hoped so.

"You must hurry. We cannot stay in these woods. Those soldiers will be back very soon. There has been a lot of fighting near here." Henri started to walk toward the woods at a fast pace.

The boys began to run to catch up. It seemed as though they ran for a long time before Henri disappeared behind some branches. He leaned around the branches and motioned for them to hurry.

They ran to join him and found themselves in a cave. After their eyes adjusted to the darkness, they could see a faint light in the distance. "My mother and sister are here. My father was captured a few days ago as we were traveling to Luxembourg to stay with my grandparents. My grandfather is sick and we were going to help take care of him and my grandmother. Now we don't know what to do. We didn't bring a lot of food with us because we knew that we would just be traveling for a day or so. I don't know where to get more food for us."

"So, were you walking to Luxembourg? I mean, how were you traveling?" Sam asked.

"We were traveling in a wagon. My father planned to stay just a few days and take my grandparents back home with us. It would be easier for them to ride in a wagon instead of walking because they are much older.

"The soldiers took our wagon, too. They left us some bread but that is all gone now. They threw off a couple of boxes that held some utensils that my mother was taking to my grandparents."

"Okay. So we don't know exactly where we are and we need to get some food. I take it that there isn't a McDonald's near here." Leon groaned as he put his face in his hands.

Henri looked at Leon with a puzzled look on his face. "I do not know what you speak of. Who is 'McDonald?' Is he a friend of yours?"

"Leon! You aren't helping any." Sam rolled his eyes. Then he placed his fist under his chin and began to rub his knuckles across his chin.

"Henri. Is there a town nearby where we can find food? Maybe Leon and I can buy some bread and cheese or something that could sustain us for a while."

"What am I supposed to do?" Billy whined.

Sam took a hold of Billy's arm. "Billy, you stay here with Henri. Maybe you can help him find some berries close by until Leon and I return."

"I don't know anything about finding berries. If I knew how to do that I wouldn't have to be hungry all the time at home.

"Wait a minute. Are there bats in this cave? I've heard that bats can suck your blood out!" Billy covered his head with his arms.

"Billy, if there were bats in here, Henri and his family would not be able to stay. There are no bats here. Calm down. We need you to help Henri," Sam explained.

Henri watched the exchange between Sam and Billy with some trepidation. As if he did not understand everything that was being said.

Henri finally looked at Sam and answered his question. "Yes. There is a small town about two miles to the east. You can walk there but you must stay in the woods. Do not get on the main road. Do you understand?"

Sam and Leon answered "yes" and left the cave.

The boys began to walk in the direction that Henri pointed out to them. Two miles to the east. They ran one mile most days to stay in shape for basketball so walking two miles should not be a problem. Coach was always telling them to "pick it up" during practice so they began to walk at a steady pace. It was hard to walk in the dense brush of the woods, but they knew they had to find food for themselves, and Billy, and Henri and his family.

After they had been walking for a short distance, Sam stopped. "Leon! Did you hear a noise? It sounded like horses in the distance. We have stayed in the woods like Henri told us to do. What do you think is going on?"

Leon stopped to listen. "You're right. I think the soldiers have come back to this area. I wonder what they are looking for."

All of a sudden there was a loud noise. Sam turned just as something whizzed by Leon's head. He fell to the ground. Was someone shooting at them? Then he heard more gunshots. "Oh snap!" Sam shouted in a loud whisper. "Get down! Those are real bullets!"

Leon flattened himself on the ground next to Sam. "We need to get out of here. If they see us they may not take us alive. Let's go beyond that row of trees and watch to see which direction they go."

Sam and Leon began to run toward the trees while crouched down to stay out of sight. They could hear bullets whizzing over their heads. Suddenly Leon dove into a clump of bushes with Sam right behind him.

Almost immediately some men on horses stopped right in front of them. Sam's heart was beating so hard that he was afraid that the men would hear the pounding in his chest. He held his breath in an attempt to calm down. He saw that Leon was doing the same thing.

The men started shouting in a language that the boys didn't understand. But then Sam recognized one of the words as a soldier shouted "Niene!" which meant "no" in German. Sam remembered the word from some of the commentaries he watched on TV.

One of the men got off his horse. He stood there a moment and then asked in English. "Did any of you see two little boys run into these bushes?"

No one answered the man. Just as the soldier turned to walk back towards the others, Leon sneezed. Sam clapped his hand over Leon's mouth. The soldier yelled "Who's there?"

The two boys froze and then they took off running along the brush line as fast as they could. They could feel the briars that snagged their clothes.

Finally Sam stopped and turned to Leon, "Do you hear anything? Are they still coming after us? Do think we got away from them?"

Leon stopped to catch his breath. "I don't hear anything. I think we should keep going and get as far away as we can."

"Which way should we go?" Sam asked.

"Any direction that is away from those soldiers!"

After they had walked a short distance, they heard a snuffling noise toward the clearing on the left. Both boys stopped and listened. It sounded like a snort coming from the open field. They leaned in and parted the bushes. There stood a large, brown horse. It even had a saddle and saddle bags. There was no one around the horse.

"Sam, why would someone leave a horse out here?"

"I don't know. Do you see anyone near the horse?"

Leon parted the bush and scanned the area with his eyes. "No. I don't see anyone around."

The boys stood watching the horse for a few minutes. Finally Sam asked Leon, "Do you know how to ride a horse?"

"No, I've never ridden a horse before. I have never even been on a farm. Do you know how to ride a horse?"

Sam sighed. "Well...I have never actually ridden a horse but I see soldiers ride horses all the time on TV. How hard can it be?"

They began to walk softly toward the horse. As they neared, the large animal lifted its head and snorted. Sam and Leon froze. After several moments the horse lowered its head and began to nibble at some grass.

Sam motioned for Leon to follow him. The horse raised its head again and looked at them. Sam whispered to the horse, "Easy. Easy, Boy!"

Leon looked at Sam and asked "Are you trying to be the 'Horse Whisperer?'" Sam shot a look at Leon and raised his finger to his lips to keep Leon from talking out loud. He didn't want to alarm the horse.

The boys kept moving slowly toward the horse. Finally, Sam reached out and touched the horse's nose. He patted it softly while he continued to whisper. Then he reached for the reigns. The horse took a step backwards as he watched Sam. The horse was much larger than it looked from over in the bushes. Sam wondered how they would get on him.

Sam stepped toward the saddle. The stirrup was higher up than he could reach with his foot. "Leon, give me a boost. When I get in the saddle I will pull you up. We can ride the horse together." Sam put his foot in Leon's hand and Leon lifted him up. Sam grabbed the saddle horn and pulled himself up. He landed in the saddle with a 'whump.' He took a couple seconds to secure his seat in the saddle and then looked down at Leon. It seemed as though Leon was a long way down.

Sam reached down his hand. "Come on, Leon. Put your foot in the stirrup, take my hand and let's get you up here." Sam held on to the saddle horn as Leon put his foot in the stirrup and reached up for Sam's hand. It took some effort, but Sam was able to pull Leon up on the horse to sit behind him and the saddle.

Leon wobbled and grabbed Sam's waist. "Don't look down, Leon. It's a long way down there." Leon looked down. "Whoa! You just had to say that, didn't you? How big is this horse? Do you know how to drive this thing?" Leon asked with a panicked voice.

"No, I don't know how to 'drive' this thing but we have to try." Sam shook the reigns but the horse just stood there. He said "Giddyup" and the horse still just stood there. "Do something before somebody sees us," Leon whispered loudly.

"I'm trying!" Sam squeezed the horse with his legs and made a clicking noise with his tongue. The horse began to walk slowly. Sam pulled the reign to the right and the horse began to walk toward the row of trees. Sam held onto the saddle horn while Leon clung to his waist. The horse's big hoofs made a plodding sound on the ground as it moved.

Sam squeezed his legs a little harder and the horse broke into a trot. "Ooh, I am going to fall off," Leon said.

"Hold on, Leon. We will get used to the up and down motion in just a few minutes. We need to get into the woods so we aren't seen by anyone. I'm afraid to go too slow. You have to admit that this is faster than walking."

"I don't know…I think I can run pretty fast on my own," Leon huffed.

They reached the tree line and then slipped into the woods. The horse seemed to know where it was going. Sam had no idea where they were so he let the horse do the leading.

After what seemed like hours had passed, the horse came into a clearing and stopped. "Why did you stop?" Leon asked.

Sam sat looking around the clearing. Before he could answer Leon, his stomach growled…loudly. He realized that it had been awhile since he had eaten breakfast. Then he heard Leon's stomach growl, too. "We need to find something to eat. I don't know about you but the Pop Tart that I ate for breakfast is long gone. I had some chips and Gatorade in my backpack but I don't have that with me," Sam stated.

"Dude, I'm hungry, too. If I had known that we were going to be lost in the woods in another country I would have packed a bag," Leon said sarcastically.

"Thanks, Leon. I appreciate your thoughtfulness." Sam sat a moment and exclaimed, "Wait a minute! There are saddlebags on this horse. Maybe there is some food in them. See if you can open one and find us some food."

"I don't know if I can reach the saddlebags without falling off the horse. Which one should I check first?" Leon asked quietly so as not to spook the horse.

"Grab hold of my shirt and look at the bag on your right. See if you can find anything. I'll hold your shirt to keep you from falling."

Leon grabbed a fistful of Sam's shirt. Then he carefully leaned over the horse. It was a long way down if he fell off. He hoped he could hold on and open the bag with one hand. He leaned over a little further. His hand found the loop on the saddlebag. Using his right hand he kept twisting the loop until he got it open. He leaned a little further while he held on to Sam's shirt. He could not see into the bag so he used his hand to feel around. Finally he found something that felt crinkly to his fingers. He grabbed the package and pulled it out of the saddlebag.

The package looked strange and he could not read the letting on it because it was in a different language. It had something that looked like crackers. He straightened up, turned loose of Sam's shirt and said, "Well, I'm not sure what we have but let me open it up. Hopefully, it will be something that we can eat."

Leon opened the package and found two crackers of a sort. He handed one to Sam and said, "Happy Eating."

Sam took a bite of the cracker and found it to be sweet. He was so hungry he believed that he could have eaten the bark off of a tree.

Leon took a bite. "Hmm. That's not too bad. It isn't Mrs. B's chocolate chunk cookies, that's for sure, but it sure beats nothing."

Sam and Leon continued to eat their crackers. They wanted to stretch it as far as they could because they did not know when they would get to eat again. Sam was a little concerned that he had no idea where they were. He was sure that they were not going in the direction that Henri had told them to go. He hadn't heard anyone following them so hopefully they were in the clear.

He continued to look around beyond the trees ahead of them. Where the horse had stopped was on a little hill and he could see over the trees. He thought he caught a glimpse of a roof in the distance.

"Leon, I think I see a roof up ahead. Do you think that is the building we're looking for?"

Leon stretched his neck to see where Sam was pointing. He caught a glimpse of the sun reflecting off of something. Then he saw the building. It looked like a hotel it was so big. But there wouldn't be a hotel in the middle of the woods. Would there? "How far away do you think that is? And can we get there from here?"

"I don't know how far it is but I don't think we have a choice. We need to get there and hope that they are friendly people. I don't like being shot at."

Sam sat looking in the distance. It would be dark soon and they had a long way to go. He was glad they had the horse but who knew what kind of terrain was between them and the building. What would happen if they could not get to that building? How long would it take them to get there? Also, it was cold. How could it be December when it was summer at home? Not too long ago he had thought how bored he was with school out for the summer. He wasn't bored now!

He prayed. "Lord, please help us to find our way out of here and to that building so we can find food for all of us. Protect us from the soldiers. Amen."

CHAPTER 9

Sam clicked his tongue and squeezed his legs. The horse began to walk. Bushes and underbrush were everywhere but the horse seemed to not have any problem walking. The air was cooler, too. Sam wished he had a jacket, but it was ninety degrees at home today.

Who knew that they would be in another time period? Maybe they could get jackets at the building they saw. He could see chill bumps on Leon's arms.

If it was 1914, then they were in World War I! Could this be the area where Captain Hornby and his troop fought a battle just a few months prior to December? What did Mr. Teddy say about Mack? Oh yes, Mack found the sword near here! No one knew whose sword Mack had found, but the sword would not be found for several years because Mack did not join the army until 1917. Wouldn't it be cool to see the sword that Mack found? Sam knew that it was not possible that he and Leon would see that sword, and if they did, would it alter the course of history?

Enough daydreaming, Sam told himself. We need to find a way to get to the building on that hill. How much further could it be? The horse continued to walk on a path that only he could see.

Leon started squirming behind him. "Leon, be still or you're going to spook the horse."

"We need to get off for a minute. I need to use the bathroom and I need to go now!"

Sam called "Whoa" to the horse and pulled back on the reins. The horse stopped. They were still in the woods so Sam was sure no one could see them there. He turned to Leon and helped him off the horse. Then Sam swung his leg over the saddle and slid off. He fell to the ground with a thud.

His legs felt like mush and his backside was sore. He finally stood up and rubbed his behind. "Whew! I think I have blisters all over my backside!" Sam exclaimed.

Leon rubbed his behind, too, and said, "I think I have blisters, too, but I can't wait any longer. I have to go now!' Leon began to run behind some bushes.

Sam stayed close to the horse so he could hold the reigns. He decided that he needed to use the bathroom, too.

It was hard to hold on to the reigns and take care of business with just one hand, but he managed to get it done. It seemed to take forever but he didn't want to let the horse wander off.

Wait a minute! Where was Leon? Did he make a turn in the trees and I didn't see him? Should I call out to him? Sam stopped to look around. Finally he called out in a loud whisper. "Leon! Where are you?" Sam heard a noise. It sounded as though it came from below him.

"Leon! Is that you?" Sam waited to listen. He heard the noise again. It sounded as though it came from beyond the trees but he couldn't tell. There was so much brush and the trees were a distance from him. Where could Leon be?

"Sam! I am down here. Can you see me? I'm in some vines and I can't get out. You're going to have to help me." Leon yelled.

Sam began walking toward Leon's voice. It sounded as though he was pretty close but he still could not see him. "Seriously Sam," Leon said grumpily, "I need some help down here. These vines are thick and I feel like I am going to choke to death."

Sam responded, "Leon, keep talking. I think I am almost there. You sound very close."

"I'm gonna keep talking! You hurry up and get here. Man, I think these vines are alive. I think one just moved up my leg," Leon shouted.

"I can see you! Did you fall? Are you hurt?" Sam asked.

Sam slid down the ravine to help Leon. He was going to have to stop daydreaming. Leon could have been hurt and he would not even have noticed. He finally saw what was holding Leon. He had slid under a huge vine. Hopefully Sam would be able to pull him out.

"Leon, are you hurt anywhere?"

"Just my pride, Dude...Just my pride." Leon said woefully, as he spit out a leaf from his mouth.

"Okay, let's see how we can get you out." Sam crawled around the area where Leon was trapped. He saw that smaller vines were crisscrossed over the larger vine. Sam peered below the large vine. There was an opening where Leon had slid into the ravine.

"Leon, if you can scoot on your back towards me, I think you can get out. Take your time and see if you can get through those smaller vines that are just above your head."

Sam watched as Leon began to scoot on his back. The smaller vines above him tried to catch at him as he wiggled around. Sam saw Leon slap at the vines like a bear swatting at honey bees. It would have been funny to watch if Leon wasn't so upset. It was a slow, tedious process for Leon but he finally got out.

Leon laid on the ground for a minute. "Dude, those vines must have been alive because they were crawling all over me. I swear I saw one wave its leaves at me."

Sam chuckled. "Man, you have a vivid imagination. I think what you saw was the wind blowing the leaves. The vine is not alive. Rest a minute and then we need to get out of here. I don't know how long it will be before it gets dark and I don't want to be caught out here after dark."

Leon finally stood up. He brushed leaves off his britches. "Have you seen the building lately? I can't seem to see anything through all of the trees."

"No, I haven't seen the building because I was looking for you. And I have gotten disoriented after being in this ravine," Sam responded.

Leon groaned as he tried to stand up. "I think I sprained my ankle. I don't know if can put any weight on it. What are we going to do?"

Sam thought for a minute. He asked himself what would happen if Leon wouldn't be able to walk.

He looked around for a branch that he could use to make a crutch for Leon. Sam found a branch that was about the right height for Leon to use. He broke the branch by beating it on a rock. After several attempts, he got the branch at the right height. Sam took it to Leon to test it.

"Leon, see if you can stand up and try out this branch. It may be strong enough for you to use. Hopefully it will last until we can get back to the horse."

Leon tried out the branch. "This will do the trick, I think," Leon said carefully. "We may have to go slow until I get the hang of using this thing. I've never used a crutch before, have you?"

"No I haven't. I sprained my ankle last year during a basketball game but I didn't have to use a crutch. Remember how I limped around for days? It was terrible. I felt like I hobbled forever. But thankfully it didn't last too long.

"Are you able to walk yet? We need to get going."

Leon tested the crutch with a few more steps. "Yeah. I can do this. I've had a few sprained ankles playing basketball myself. I'll be okay. Let's go."

The boys began to walk through the underbrush until they reached the horse. Sam was able to get his foot in the stirrup and pull himself up then help Leon up on the horse.

Just as the horse started walking, Sam pulled on the reigns. "Did you hear that?"

"It sounded like an alarm." Leon strained to listen. "No…a bell! What do you think it is?"

"I don't know but it sounded like it came just beyond that thicket up ahead. Let's see if we can get through this brush. I hope the horse can get through there because I'm not sure that you could walk that far with your sprained ankle."

Leon sat for a moment as he looked into the distance. "Yeah. Let's keep going. I don't think I'm up to a lot of walking."

Sam put his hand on Leon's shoulder. "Then, let's do this."

~ ~ ~

The horse moved slowly through the thicket. Sam and Leon tried to keep the building in their view, but the trees would get in the way of their vision. It felt as though they had been riding forever, and it felt like they were not getting any closer to the building.

The night air was getting cooler. Sam wished again that he had on a jacket. He could hear Leon's teeth chattering. In fact, his teeth were chattering, too.

They didn't talk because they didn't want anyone to hear them. A twig snapped!

The horse stopped, then took off at a gallop. Both boys held on tight. "Whoa! Stop him, Sam!"

"I'm trying! Hold on, Leon!"

Both boys held on for their lives. The horse continued to gallop at a fast pace. They had to duck as they went under tree branches. Dusk was all around them and it was hard to see. They could only hope that the horse could see where he was going.

Sam looked around to check on Leon and when he did a tree branch caught him on the side of the head. Sam fell off the horse and on to the ground with a thump. Leon was pulled off with him. Both boys lay on the ground panting and shaking.

The horse stopped a few yards away. It was covered with flecks of foam. Its sides were heaving from all the exertion. The horse turned and looked at the boys and nickered, as if to ask if they were okay.

Sam looked over at Leon. "Are you okay? I didn't see that branch."

Leon moaned. "Yeah, I'm okay. What a rough way to get off a horse."

After a few more minutes of resting, the boys got up. They walked over to the horse. "Wonder what spooked him?" Leon asked as he stood watching the horse.

"I don't know but I think we need to let him rest. I remember seeing a show on TV that when a horse sweats like this that it needs to rest. Maybe we aren't too far away from that building and we can make it on foot. Do you think your ankle is up to walking?"

"I guess I don't have a choice now except to walk on it. You're right that the horse needs to rest and dry off.

Everything happened so fast that I didn't see the building but maybe it won't be too far off."

The boys looked around for something that could be used as a crutch for Leon. Sam finally found a branch that could be used. It wasn't as good as the one they had before, but it would work. He took it back to Leon and with Sam's help, Leon was able to hobble along.

Sam prayed that the building wasn't too far away. They were cold, tired, and hungry, and he could tell that Leon's foot bothered him more than he was letting on.

« CHAPTER 10 »

Billy did not like being in the cave. The fire in the center of the room cast weird shadows on the walls. Henri had been friendly toward him, but the woman and the little girl just stared at him. He smiled at the little girl and she half-smiled back at him. He still worried that there might be bats in the cave. He had seen a documentary on TV about bats and how they could get in your hair. Billy reached up to touch his hair. It was long and shaggy. Maybe he should think about getting a haircut when he got home.

Home. He had thought many times these past few months that he wished he could run away and go to his grandma's house. His mom had been drunk more than she had been sober this past year and he had gotten where he didn't like to be around her. Now he would be glad to be home and not here…wherever *here* was. He shivered. Even though the fire was warm he could not get warm. He felt a chill go through his bones.

Henri laid a blanket over him. "I'm sorry you are so cold." Henri told him. "My mother wants you to have her blanket. Everything will look better tomorrow. Perhaps your friends will return with some food."

His friends. They weren't his friends. He didn't have friends. He made sure of that by acting out in class and picking on the other kids. He was afraid that if he became friendly with the others that they would want to come to his house. He couldn't let anyone come to his house, not with his mom drinking like she did. He didn't even have a play station or any other games like the other kids. They couldn't afford anything like that. Tears rolled down his cheeks as he thought about his home life. He wiped his face with his sleeve. There was nothing he could do about that. Not now. Maybe not ever. He sure hoped he could go home soon.

His mind kept going back to the little room and the flash of light. What had happened? How did they get back to 1914? This was very weird and he had no answer to his own questions. His head was filled with images of the flash of light.

~~~

"Oh, Mom, just let me sleep a while longer," Billy mumbled. He rolled over to find Henri looking at him strangely. He sat up quickly. He was not at home. He was still in the cave. He fell back to the ground. It wasn't a dream. He was really in a cave in the middle of…well, he wasn't really sure where he was at this moment.

"You need to eat, Billy. We have a few berries but that will have to do until your friends return with food."

Billy looked around. The woman and little girl were huddled together and they were eating berries out of their hand. Henri held out his hand so Billy could get some berries. Billy reached for the berries, and then pulled back his hand. "Do you have enough berries for you, Henri?"

"Yes, I have already eaten. These are for you."

Billy took the berries and popped them into his mouth. They were bitter but he was glad to have them. His stomach was so empty that the berries only seemed to make him more hungry. He had more to eat at home than berries. Oh how he wished he was at home now. A cold Pop Tart would taste better than these sour berries.

He stood up and folded the blanket. Then he sat back down. What was he supposed to do now? He could not stay here with these people and eat their food. There weren't enough berries for four people and how long could they last on just berries?

"Henri, when was the last time that you and your family had something to eat? I mean, real food, to eat?"

"It has been a few days. When the soldiers took my daddy, they took our wagon which had our food in it. I have tried to find food but berries are the only thing I could find. We won't be able to find berries much longer due to the cold weather. I don't know what we can do."

Billy sat for a few minutes. Surely there was something more that they could find to eat. There wasn't a grocery store that they could walk to like he could at home. He looked at his shoes. What if he took a shoe lace and made a snare of some type where they could catch a bird or some other animal to eat? If they were near a creek he could catch fish. His daddy had taught him how to make a snare when he led the Boy Scout troop. Of course, that was a couple years ago before he died. Billy wasn't even sure that he could remember how to make a snare but he had to try. These people would starve to death if he didn't do something.

Billy began looking around the room where they slept to see if he could find anything else useful. He noticed Henri watching his every move. When he caught Henri's eyes, Henri asked, "What are you looking for? Are you going to rob us?"

"What? No! I am not going to rob you. I'm looking to see if there is anything we can use to make a snare to catch a small animal or even a bird. You can't keep living on just berries. You have to have something more."

Henri sighed. "I know. I'm supposed to be the man of the family now that my father isn't here, but I don't know how to find food for them. Do you have any ideas?"

"Well, I was in the Boy Scouts and I was taught how to make a snare. My dad taught me that before he died. It has been a while since I made one but I think I can still remember how. I can use a shoe lace and we will need some sticks. Do you have anything that I can use for rags?"

"Boy Scouts? Who are they?"

"It is a group for boys where they can learn survival tips. I haven't been to a meeting in over a year. Not since my dad died." Billy stopped talking.

Henri stood and looked around the room. He went over and spoke to his mother in a language that Billy didn't understand. The woman shook her head "no" and shrugged her shoulders. The little girl nudged her mother and then she began to speak. The mother looked at the little girl, and then nodded "yes". The little girl lifted her skirt. Billy watched with fascination as she began to tear strips from her undergarment. She looked at Billy after she had torn off several strips. He nodded to her that it was good. She smiled shyly at him as she handed the strips of cloth to Henri.

Henri then gave the strips to Billy. He took the strips and began walking toward the opening in the cave. Henri came bounding up behind him. "What are you going to do?" he asked Billy.

Billy stopped and turned to face Henri. "I'm going to build a snare. Stay here. I need to do this by myself."

Billy went out of the cave. He looked in all directions. "I wonder where would be a good place to put a snare," he thought to himself.

As he continued to look around he noticed a clump of grass beneath some bushes. He pondered how a small rabbit or squirrel could hide in the clump of thick grass. Billy went over to the bushes. He got down on his knees and looked underneath to see if he could see evidence of a small animal having been there. He parted the branches on the bush and there was grass that had been tamped down as if something had slept there.

He found some twigs and he set to work with his shoelaces and the strips of cloth from the little girl's under garment. The first couple of times he tried the snare, it would not work. Billy sighed in frustration. What was he doing wrong? He just knew that he was making the snare like his dad taught him!

Billy sat back on his heels and surveyed the layout of his snare. He prayed, "God, I want to help these people find food but I'm not sure that I have built this right. Please help me."

Then he berated himself for praying. Billy didn't want to believe in a God that would take his daddy from him. He was just nine years old when his daddy died. He needed a daddy. If God was a loving God then why would he leave a little boy without a father? He wiped his brow on his sleeve. He sighed in frustration again. The snare had to work…it just had to!

Billy went back into the cave. Henri and his sister looked to be playing a game. The mother sat huddled up in a blanket. She had a look like his momma had sometimes…blank. How much longer would he be here, he wondered. And when were Sam and Leon coming back? He layed down on the floor. All they could do was wait.

~~~

"Billy! Wake up!" Henri was shaking him. Billy sat up. Henri was holding a small rabbit in his hand. The snare worked! It actually worked!

The mother was talking excitedly and moving her hands up and down. Billy looked at Henri. "What is she saying?" he asked Henri.

Henri looked at Billy and grinned. "She said to 'clean it and she will cook it over the fire.'"

The boys went out of the cave. Henri went toward a small brook to clean the small rabbit. Billy went to re-set the snare. He saw the little girl go toward the trees.

After Billy finished with the snare he went to check on Henri. "Do you need some help?" he asked.

Henri looked up with a grin and said, "Yes. Hold him while I pull the skin." Billy knelt down and gripped the rabbit in his hand. It was hard to get a good grip but he finally got it. Henri used his knife to cut the skin. He laid the knife down and with both hands he pulled the skin toward him.

Henri tugged until the skin was completely off, then he told Billy to pull the other half of the skin toward him. Billy pulled while Henri held his end of the rabbit. Billy had forgotten what a skinned rabbit looked like. It didn't look like much meat but he hoped it would taste good. Henri rinsed the rabbit in the brook. Then he slit open the stomach and removed the insides of the rabbit. He rinsed the rabbit again.

"I think we have cleaned it enough. Momma will know what to do with it now," Henri told Billy.

When they went into the cave, the mother had a pot of boiling water hanging over the fire. Green leaves floated in the water. Henri handed the rabbit to his mother. She took the rabbit from him and held it in her hands. She looked to be praying over the rabbit. She cut the rabbit into small pieces and put it into the boiling water. Then she sat back and waited.

Henri sat next to Billy. "We are going to have rabbit stew. Mia," he pointed to his sister, "found some herbs to put in the stew. Momma can make anything taste good. I can hardly wait. Anything will be better than berries." Henri grinned at him. They continued to sit and watch the pot. Billy could hear his grandmother say, "A watched pot never boils."

Mia sat next to her mother and they talked quietly. Mia giggled softly at something her mother said. Henri looked at them and grinned. It was the first time he had heard Mia and Momma talking since they had been left at the cave. He was glad Billy was left behind with them.

The mother stood up and so did Mia. The mother gestured toward their pack. Mia went over and pulled out some small bowls and spoons. She handed them to the mother where she poured some stew into each of the bowls. Mia handed one of the bowls to Billy, and then Henri and she sat down with a bowl. The mother took a bowl and then bowed her head. Billy bowed and listened as the mother prayed. He didn't understand anything she said but he heard "Danke" several times. It sounded like "thank you" and felt that she was thanking God for the rabbit stew.

When she finished praying she took a bite of the stew then nodded for them to eat. Billy tentatively brought the spoon to his mouth to taste the stew. He watched as

Henri and Mia took a bite. He took a bite and was surprised to find that the stew was very tasty. The meat tasted like the dark meat of chicken. The mother, Mia and Henri smiled after eating several spoonfuls.

The mother said something to Henri as she pointed to Billy. Henri looked at Billy and translated, "Momma says that you are a smart boy. She says that we would have starved if you had not made the snare that trapped the rabbit. Thank you, Billy, for helping us."

Billy felt his face get warm. He wasn't used to anyone telling him that he had done something good. It gave him a good feeling. Mia walked over and sat next to him. She looked at him and laid her arm on his sleeve. "Thank you, Billy, for finding food for us," she whispered.

After the meal Mia took the bowls and utensils out to clean them in the brook. Henri went with her to watch over her. Billy went out to reset the snare. Hopefully they would get another rabbit that the mother could cook for them.

When they returned to the cave they went to bed for the night. Billy fell asleep thinking about the good feeling he had for helping Henri's family.

« CHAPTER 11 »

The building could be seen in the distance. Sam could not tell what type of building it was, but it appeared to be fairly large. He hoped that they had some food because he was starving and he knew that Leon was, too.

Leon paused for a moment. His ankle bothered him some, but the crutch helped to relieve some of the stress on his ankle as he walked. He was glad that the building was not too far away because he didn't know how much further he would be able to walk.

The boys started moving forward again. Sam began to wonder if there would be soldiers at the building. They would need to look for a way to get in without being seen.

"Sam, look!" Leon whispered. "There are soldiers!"

Sam saw them. Were these the same guys that were chasing them earlier? Were they German soldiers? Or English soldiers? They needed to find a place to hide and they needed to find it now.

They crept around to the east side of the building. Sam saw a window near the ground. He motioned to Leon that they needed to go over to the window. Maybe it would be open and they could get into the building that way.

They crawled up to the window. Leon pushed against it with his shoulder. It was not locked! It moved with a loud creak. Sam and Leon froze. Was it loud enough to be heard? They looked to see if anyone was around. They didn't' see anyone so Leon pushed again. It was a small opening so it was going to be tough to get through to the inside. Leon looked at Sam and said, "Sam, you're shorter than I am so you crawl through and see if you can get the window to open more."

"Me? You want me to crawl in there? You know I don't like small spaces!" Sam whined.

"Sam! It won't be a small space after you get through the window. Look! There is a room on the other side," Leon responded urgently.

Sam sighed. "Okay. I'm not sure that being shorter is a good reason for me to be the one to go through the window first. Here, help me hold the window open."

Sam stuck his head through the window. Leon was right. There was a room. Now if he could just get through the window without being caught. "Okay. I can do this." Sam thought to himself. He went in head first. Unfortunately, he did not realize that the floor was several feet below the window. He hit the floor with a thud, but he was able to roll so he did not land on his head.

"Are you okay?" Leon whispered loudly.

"Yeah. I'm okay. Leon, you're going to have to come through the window backwards. I will hold onto your legs so you won't hit the floor too hard. You don't want to hurt your sprained ankle," Sam explained.

"Okay." Leon wriggled around until his legs went through the window. Sam grabbed hold of Leon's legs.

"You have a couple feet before you get to the floor. I will hold you but you need to come in slowly so I don't drop you. Got it?" Sam said while he held onto Leon.

All of a sudden Leon fell on top of Sam and they both hit the floor. Sam felt the breath go out of his lungs with a loud whoosh! Leon just laid there. Great! Now what!

"Sam, are you okay? Did I hurt you? I didn't mean to fall. My hands slipped and I couldn't hold on. Answer me!"

"I'm okay, Leon. The fall just knocked the breath out of me. Are you okay? Did you hurt your sprained ankle?"

Leon stood up. His ankle felt fine...no worse than before. He hobbled a little and turned around to help Sam off the floor. Sam stood up and walked around and bounced on his feet.

"I'm okay. Whew! That could have been a lot worse. Let's look around to see if there is a way out of this room," Sam stated.

As their eyes adjusted to the semi-darkness, they could see objects in the room. In fact, one of the objects looked to be covered with a sheet. They couldn't tell if it was a table or a bed but it was a long shape. Like a bed.

"Sam, what do you think is under that sheet? Should we take a look?"

"I don't think we need to look under that sheet. I'm not so sure of what we would find. Wait. I see some stairs in the corner and there is a door at the top of the stairs. Let's see where it goes," Sam whispered.

~~~

Sam pushed the door open and peeked through to see a long hallway. Then he saw a woman wearing a white dress with a white cap on her head. Sam closed the door. "Leon! We are in a hospital!"

"A hospital! There are probably soldiers here. We need to make sure that we aren't seen by any of them. Do you see anyone now?" Leon asked.

Sam opened the door a small crack. He looked both ways in the hall. It was empty. He motioned for Leon to follow him. They began walking down a long corridor. The lights were dim and it was very quiet.

They slipped into the dimly lit hallway. Leon pantomimed that they should go to the end of the hallway to see where it would lead. They tiptoed quietly. When they reached the end of the hallway they saw that it went both directions. They looked to the left and then to the right.

Leon limped alongside of Sam. "Where do you think the food would be? I'm hungry." His stomach growled as if to confirm the hunger.

"I'm beginning to think that all you think about is food. But you're right. I'm hungry too! Let's see what we can find."

Sam pointed to a sign at the end of the hallway to the left. The sign was in a foreign language and they could not read it. Sam jerked his head to the left to indicate that they should go that way. He and Leon began to walk toward the sign. Just as they passed a doorway a hand reached out and grabbed Sam by the sleeve.

~~~

Sam let out a yelp. Then he heard "Ssh!" He turned to look at who just shushed him. It was a small girl. She had on a white dress with a red cross on the pinafore. She wore a white cap on her head. She had dark hair and dark eyes. She was shorter than Sam. She did not smile.

"Uh, hello." Leon began to say. The little girl put her finger over her lips to indicate that they would need to be quiet. She stepped into the hallway and looked both directions then she went back into the room and shut the door.

Sam and Leon looked at each other. Sam began, "Do you speak English?" He patted his chest and said, "I am Sam." He pointed to Leon. "His name is Leon."

The little girl pointed to herself and said, "I am Anna. Good to meet you. Yes, I speak some English. What are you doing here?"

Leon stuttered, "Well, we, uh, well, we were…"

Sam stared at Leon. "We were lost in the forest and saw this building from a distance. We were hoping to find some food for us and for our friends who are hiding out in a cave. Is this a hospital?" He asked Anna.

"Yes, this is a hospital. I am a VAD and I work here on the weekends."

"You're a what?" Sam asked with a quizzical look.

"We are called VADs which means 'Voluntary Aid Detachments'. We were formed by the Red Cross and the order of St. John. We are here to administer first aid to the patients, we take them to surgery when needed, and sometimes we have to transport the patients to other facilities when they leave here.

"Come, I will show you where to get some food, but we need to stay quiet so we don't get caught."

Anna led them down the hallway and took a right at the end. All the hallways were very confusing as they all looked the same to Sam and Leon. Suddenly there was a troop of soldiers coming toward them. Anna opened a door and said, "Quick! Duck in here where the soldiers cannot see you."

They were in a small closet with brooms and mops. Leon grabbed his nose. "Man, it smells terrible in here? What is that smell?"

Anna looked confused. She picked up a mop and said, "You smell cleaning fluids. We have to keep the floors clean to prevent the smell of blood and death in the hospital. The clean floors also keep diseases from being spread among the patients. Wounded soldiers are brought here for us to care for and help them recover. Many have lost an arm or a leg. It is horrible." She said as tears formed in her eyes. She opened the door. "It's safe now. Let's go."

Sam and Leon followed Anna to the door. She gasped! She quickly pushed them back into the closet and shut the door. Sam saw a blur of movement and Anna curtsey just as the door closed. He wondered what, or who, she saw that made her react so mysteriously.

They stayed in the closet for what seemed like an eternity. Suddenly the door knob began to turn. Sam and Leon squeezed into the corner and hoped that no one saw them. They both sighed with relief when they saw Anna's head pop around the door. She motioned for them to follow her. Again they made their way to the end of another hallway and turned toward the left.

Anna stopped at a door. She turned to them and motioned for them to stay quiet. She opened the door and they saw a curtain hanging there. They walked into the room and once again she put her finger over her lips for them to be quiet. Then she pulled back the curtain.

On the bed was a young man who had a bandage wrapped around his head. His left leg looked strange. There was a bloody bandage around his knee, but there was nothing below the knee. His leg was missing. His right leg was also bandaged around the knee but his leg stuck out below the bandage. Both boys just stared. Then they heard a voice speaking in a low tone.

Sam could not believe his eyes. He saw a woman sitting beside the bed. She presented the young man a box and said, "I know that you wanted to go back to the field. I am very sorry about your leg. I have brought you a small gift."

Sam gasped as he saw what she handed the soldier. It was a brass box! The same brass box that Beth had shown to the group. Beth had asked him to put it on the shelf, which he attempted to do before he fell.

Sam asked himself, "Did the box send us back to this time?" The man opened the box and began to pull out the contents. There was a writing pen, a small tablet, and some chocolate.

The man spoke to the lady, but the boys did not understand what he said. Tears rolled down his face. The nurse that stood at attention handed him a cloth which he used to wipe the dampness off his face.

The woman by the bed took the soldier's hand. Her small hand barely covered the back of the man's large hand. She looked at him and said, "I am so proud of you for the service you have given to our country. It is brave men like you who protect us. It is never our intent that anyone be harmed in any way but, unfortunately, these things happen in a war. While we are aware of the tragedies of war, it doesn't make it any easier to accept or understand."

The young man looked at the woman again. "It is my honor to serve my country, Your Royal Highness. I would go back if they would let me, but, alas, there isn't much that a one-legged soldier can do on the battlefield."

"You have already given so much. Please get word to me if you need anything. Anyone on the staff here at the hospital will know how to reach me. Again, I am sorry for your injuries. I will keep you in my prayers."

The woman got up from her chair. When she turned around, she looked at Sam and smiled. It was Princess Mary of England! He recognized her because he had seen pictures of her on the internet. He had just witnessed

Princess Mary giving a Christmas present to the young soldier!

Princess Mary said, "I have sent these boxes to the men on the front lines, but I wanted to give you one personally. It is just a small token of appreciation."

Anna pushed Sam and Leon out of the room. It seemed to Sam that time had stood still while they were in the small room. Leon looked at Sam with a weird expression on his face.

"Did you know who that woman was? I heard you suck in your breath when she looked at you. And she smiled at you as if she knew you!," exclaimed Anna.

Sam looked at Leon. Then he looked at Anna. "I, I just saw…" Sam hesitated, took a deep breath and swallowed. He began again. "That was Princess Mary. Wasn't it? She came to this hospital to visit that soldier. Did she visit other soldiers at this hospital? Does she visit patients here very often? I mean, will we see her again?" Sam stopped talking. His mind had a hard time trying to compute what he just saw.

Anna stared at Sam. He acted so strangely. Surely he had seen Princess Mary before. Her picture was everywhere. Everyone knew who Princess Mary was.

"Yes. That woman was Princess Mary. She comes to the hospital every few months to visit with wounded soldiers. Why did you act so surprised to see her?"

Sam did not know how he was going to answer her question. Then he said, "We are not from this area. I have seen pictures of Princess Mary, but I did not expect to see her in person. Thank you for taking us to that room. I feel like we have just witnessed a very important historical event."

Anna looked at Sam and then said in a small voice. "Come. Follow me. I will find you some food. I will also find you some clothes. Your clothes are very strange and you don't even have proper coats to wear. The hospital keeps clothes in storage for emergencies."

~~~

When Anna left them to find some food and clothes, they decided to look around the hospital until they had to meet Anna in the basement.

Sam looked at Leon. "You do realize the significance of what we just witnessed with Princess Mary. Don't you?"

"Well, I'm not sure if I understood everything that she said, but she sure was a beautiful woman. Did you see her clothes? I mean, you could tell that she belonged to royalty. I mean, my mom dresses nice, but WOW! Princess Mary, she rocked, man!"

"Let me explain some of what we just witnessed." Sam began to speak in hushed tones. "According to the history of World War I, Princess Mary gave a brass box to all the soldiers who were on the front lines. Some of the boxes contained a pipe, one ounce of tobacco and 20 cigarettes. She also sent boxes for the ones who did not smoke. Those boxes contained a pencil, a writing pad and some sweets. These boxes were sent to all British officers and sailors for Christmas.

"She was able to send these boxes through a project that was called 'Princess Mary's Christmas Gift Fund'. She funded most of the money from her own personal funds for the project, but there were others who donated to help her make those brass boxes a reality.

"She sure was an awesome lady. And now we have witnessed her give a brass box to a wounded soldier. It looked just like the box that Beth showed us. I'm still trying to wrap my head around all this..." Sam's voice trailed off as he continued to think about what they had seen.

"Young man, I don't know how you know about Princess Mary and what she has done, but I am impressed with your knowledge."

Sam and Leon gasped at the same time and both whirled around to see who was talking to them. Where did this man come from? They thought they were alone.

Sam swallowed hard. "Well, sir, I guess I heard about Princess Mary at school."

"Well, that is an interesting school you must go to because most people don't know about this yet. There hasn't even been a formal announcement made to the public about Princess Mary's involvement in these gifts. Now, where do you boys come from because I know from your accent that you don't live in this area."

Leon looked at Sam. He cocked his eyebrow as if to say, "Now what?"

Sam replied, "Well, sir, Leon," he gestured toward Leon to indicate who he was, "and I are here visiting some friends. We are from the United States. Not to be rude, but your accent doesn't sound like some of the others we have heard while we have been here."

The gentleman laughed. "Young lads, if I told you the name of the small town where I came from, well, I can assure you that you have never heard of it. I, too, come from the United States.

"I was sent here to further my medical career by working with the surgical team during the war." The man's voice almost faded as he said, "I have seen a lot of tragedy while I have been here. I would like to go back home where I wouldn't have to see any more war injuries…"

His voice grew stronger as he said, "I am going to miss my family at Christmas but we all have to make sacrifices for the sake of the war."

Leon decided that they should change the subject so he asked, "So where are you from in the United States? Sam and I are from a small community in Elkton, Tennessee. That is where we go to school."

The man reared back on his heels. "Elkton? Tennessee? Lads, that is too much of a coincidence…I am from Pulaski. We are practically neighbors. I am W. J. Johnson. Some of the doctors here call me 'Doctor J'.

"Other people just call me "Doc". Now you told me Leon's name, what is yours?" he asked as he turned to Sam.

"I am Sam." He shook hands with Doc. "Sir, I would like to thank you for what you are doing over here. You have made our country proud and us, too. Because of your service to our country, we have a freedom that so many countries do not have. So, thank you for that."

Doc's eyes misted over. "Son, I don't know when I have ever been more proud. Thank you for your kind words. Now I must continue on with my rounds. God speed and safe travels when you go home. I will try to look you up when I get home to Pulaski. It's hard to believe that we have come across the pond to meet each other." Doc smiled, turned and walked toward the end of the hallway.

Sam watched as the young doctor walked away. "Leon, you do realize that Doc will not be alive by the time we return home? It will be one hundred and four years later."

"I don't want to hear that. He is such a nice man…I hope he makes it home. We will need to remember to ask our parents if they knew of him."

"We better hurry," Sam said. "We are supposed to meet Anna and I don't know how long she has been gone."

The boys took off to the other end of the hallway. They hoped they were going in the right direction. All the hallways looked the same. After they turned a corner, they saw the door to the basement. Anna was coming toward them.

"I found food and clothes. You must hurry before it gets dark. The soldiers change guard soon and they always do an inspection around the hospital. You don't want them to catch you lurking around."

They took the articles from Anna. Leon smiled shyly and said, "Thank you, Anna. You have been very kind to us. I hope you have a long life."

Anna looked at him skeptically, but said, "You are very welcome, Leon. I hope you have a long life, too. Now hurry." They stood at the door and watched her leave.

After Sam and Leon ate their food and changed their clothes, they knew that it was time to leave. They filled their coat pockets with food that Anna had gotten for them to take to Henri and his family. They only hoped that they could find the cave again. And Billy.

CHAPTER 12

They were walking through the woods and Leon remarked, "I sure am glad that Anna found us these warm clothes and coats. I will admit, though, that I never thought that I would be wearing fur around my face. And these pants are strange. They look like something that I have seen in old books. Don't you think they look kinda weird? Now that I think about it, you have been acting weird ever since you saw that woman in the hospital. What happened back there?"

Sam stopped walking. "Leon, that woman was Princess Mary of England. She was very generous to soldiers during World War I. That brass box that she gave to that soldier was one of thousands that she gave to soldiers during Christmas in 1914. In fact, I remember reading that over 400,000 of those brass boxes were given out on Christmas Day. She was a very generous woman.

"When she looked at me it felt as though she knew who I was, but I know that is impossible. I guess it felt that way because I was reading about her after Mr. Teddy told us the story about the brass box.

"I know these clothes look strange, but that is how they dressed back then. I mean, that was over 100 years ago. I think that I like the loose pants…they actually remind me of some that I wear at home. At least the pockets are deep and we were able to put extra food in the pockets for Henri and his family."

"Speaking of Henri, are you sure this is the way to the cave? I remember that we ran in a lot of directions when we were running from those soldiers. I don't remember seeing any of this before. It's all a blur to me now. What are we going to do if we can't find Henri? And what about Billy? I'm sure he has driven Henri and his family crazy with his foolishness. That boy could drive anyone crazy. You know how he is!"

"Leon! Get a grip on yourself! "I don't know if this is the right way or not. I think we need to keep walking in this direction. We know the hospital is to our backs so we must be headed in the right direction. Let's go a little further and see if we can find some landmarks that we recognize. We just have to hope that Billy is okay and that he hasn't been a nuisance. Maybe he stayed in a corner and out of the way."

The boys continued to walk without talking. Sam's mind was still swirling from his encounter with Princess Mary. How would anyone ever believe that he saw her? He wished that he could have talked to her but somehow that wasn't supposed to happen. He believed that just by witnessing her give that brass box to the soldier was all that he was supposed to do. Maybe he could tell Mr. Teddy what had happened. Mr. Teddy would not think that he was crazy, especially after he explained everything to him.

Suddenly Leon stopped. "Ssh, listen. I think I hear something walking in those bushes. We need to hide in case there are some soldiers coming toward us." They jumped behind some trees and watched to see what was moving around in the bushes.

A horse walked out of the bushes and toward them. It was their horse! The one they had been riding earlier in the day. They could not believe that the horse had stayed close. Sam and Leon walked toward the horse. Sam began to whisper to him in a soft voice. The horse continued to stand still.

"Well, are you ready to ride again?" Sam asked Leon.

"I think so. It would give my ankle some relief. It may be hard on my backside but I think I can manage."

The boys got up on the horse. They sat there for a minute to get their bearings. Sam squeezed his knees and made a clicking noise with his tongue. The horse began to walk. It was completely dark in the woods without street lights to guide them. It was also a little spooky because they couldn't see if anyone was watching them.

~ ~ ~

"Halt! Who goes there?" A loud voice boomed in the darkness.

Sam and Leon froze. The horse stopped at the sound of the loud command.

"I'll ask ye again. Who goes there? If you do not answer me I will be forced to shoot you."

"Well, uh, Sir, I am Sam. And I'm Leon." The boys answered quickly.

Suddenly a bright light was shining in their faces. "What are you lads doing out here in the middle of the night? Who are you working for? Come now, speak up."

Leon elbowed Sam in the ribs. Sam jumped, but he answered the man. "Sir, we are trying to find our friend. We left him in a cave with a family and now we need to get him so we can go home."

"And where is home, Lad?"

"We are from the United States. We were sent to visit with some friends and we have gotten lost." Sam replied.

"Whose horse is this? Do you have any papers on you explaining who you are and who you're visiting? Everyone who enters this country must have papers."

Both boys were silent. Sam looked at Leon. Leon looked back at him with an expression of "What now?"

"Well, um, uh, Sir, we, uh found this horse in a clearing earlier today. We then rode it across the fields and through the woods until we came upon a hospital. A young woman gave us some food and clothes and sent us on our way. We don't have any papers." Sam began to explain.

"You lads will have to come with us." He whistled and two soldiers stood at attention by his side. The man looked to his left and told him to take the 'Lad on the front'. "You, soldier, take the lad on the back. These boys will be going to camp with us," the man told them.

Both soldiers reached up at the same time and pulled the boys off the horse. They carried them with them to some horses that the boys had not noticed in the darkness. They were plopped down on the horses. The soldiers climbed on in front of them. The man got on another horse. He held the reigns of their horse and began to lead the way.

What was going to happen to them now?

~ ~ ~

It seemed as though they had been traveling for hours when they saw a clearing with tents in a cluster. The man told the soldiers to 'Halt''. The horses stopped.

The soldiers stayed on their horses while the man got off his horse. He handed the reigns of both horses to another soldier and then walked toward a tent at the far end of the camp. The soldiers sat quietly without speaking. The boys did, too.

After a few minutes, the man came back to the horses. "Get down and bring the boys with you. Lieutenant Grace wants to question these lads."

Sam and Leon were taken off the horses. Both of them were afraid that they would not be able to stand up. They had been riding for a while and their knees trembled like jelly.

The soldiers punched them in the back to get them started walking. Leon tried to walk without limping, but his ankle was bothering him. He didn't want the soldier to punch him again so he started walking. The tent looked like it was a football field away, but it only took a few minutes to get reach the tent.

A soldier was standing outside the tent. He opened the flap for them to enter. Sam and Leon were nudged to go first. Sam felt like he was facing a firing squad. He didn't know what to expect. Would he and Leon be kept as prisoners of war? They didn't know anything about the war! Well, only what they had studied in history and saw on the History Channel. Sam prayed, "Oh God, please help us!"

There was a soft glow in the tent as it was lit with several lanterns. In the center of the tent was a small fire pit with a fire burning. A man was sitting behind a desk. He stood up and came around the desk. He was a tall man. His hair was dark and his eyes seemed to penetrate down to their souls when he looked at them. Sam and Leon began to shiver from sheer fright.

"Laddies, why don't you stand over here next to the fire? You must be cold after riding on the back of the horses. My man tells me that you are from the United States and that you don't have the proper papers to travel through here. Would you care to explain why you are here?"

Leon looked at Sam and nodded for him to speak up. Sam looked up at the tall man standing in front of him and began to speak.

"Sir, to be honest, we are not sure where we are. We had been staying with some friends and we got separated.

Then we found a family of a woman, and a small boy and girl who were living in a cave. They didn't have anything but berries to eat." Sam nodded toward Leon and said, "My friend and I went to look for food for them. We stayed in the bushes and then we found a horse to ride.

"We came upon a hospital and a little girl there gave us some food and clothes. She was a volunteer at the hospital. She told us that the hospital keeps extra clothes for emergencies.

"Then we left and started riding again to try to find the cave where the family lived." Sam stopped talking. He felt as though he had been rambling and not making sense of anything he said.

The man watched them for a moment and then he went to his desk. He fiddled with some knobs on a radio. There was some loud static as he turned the knobs. Then the radio was quiet. He picked up a microphone from the desk and began to speak. "This is Lieutenant Thomas Marshall Grace. Is anyone there.?"

A voice spoke up. "Yes, I am here Lieutenant Grace. How can I help you, Sir?"

The lieutenant spoke for several minutes while he explained about the boys that his men had found in the field. Then he asked, "Do you know of a family in a cave? These boys told me that they are trying to find the cave and rescue the family."

"No, Sir. No one here knows anything about that but we will dispatch some soldiers to see if they can locate the family. We don't know anything about the young lads, Sir. Perhaps they are just two innocent lads who got lost in the woods?"

"Quite right, Soldier. I believe that is the case. Thanks for your assistance. Signing off now." And Lieutenant Grace clicked off the microphone and set it back on the desk..

"Well, boys, it appears that no one knows anything about you or a family living in a cave. I can't just let you wander around in the woods by yourselves, so we will let you stay in the camp tonight and tomorrow we will see if we can find your friends."

The lieutenant turned to one of the soldiers. "Private, put these boys in the tent next to mine. Get them some food and blankets. Then let them rest tonight."

"Yes, Sir!" The soldier saluted and then led the boys out of the tent and pointed to the next tent. "You will stay in there tonight. I will get you some food and then you need to get in the sleeping bags and sleep tonight. You need to stay quiet so don't be making any noise in there."

The soldier left. Leon looked over at Sam and whispered. "What are we going to do? We can't stay here. We need to find Billy and Henri. We need to see if we can get out of here.

"That Lieutenant Grace must be some important dude if he gives the orders around here."

Sam sat for a few minutes. He was trying to process the lieutenant's name. Sam remembered reading about a

Thomas Marshall Grace who was a second lieutenant in the British Army. Lieutenant

Grace had won several medals during his service to the British Army, but he was killed in action the next year after the war started. If Sam remembered his history correctly, and he was sure that he did, he lieutenant was in his mid-twenties when he died.

It made Sam sad because he really liked the lieutenant. He seemed nice and appeared to care about their welfare. At least he didn't order them to be shot.

Before Sam could say anything, the soldier returned with food. He saw the boys sitting together and said, "Now remember what I told you earlier. You need to stay quiet tonight. No talking! I will see you in the morning. So eat up and then get to sleep."

Sam and Leon ate the small portion of food that was given to them. As they sat eating, Sam whispered to Leon about what he remembered about the Lieutenant.

"Oh man, that is so sad," Leon whispered.

Sam could only nod.

They finished their meal. Sam nudged Leon and said, "You're right. We can't stay here in this camp. Let's wait awhile until everyone in the camp has settled down and then we need to leave. I have no clue where we are, but we need to get out of here as soon as possible."

"How are we going to do that when there are soldiers everywhere? Are we just gonna walk out the way we came in? And what about our horse?"

"Did you notice the small tear in the back of this tent?" Sam turned and pointed at the rip. "I believe we can slip out through there. We can't get the horse. It will be too risky and too noisy. We will have to walk out of here."

Leon sat a minute and then nodded his agreement. Both boys laid down on their sleeping bags. They could not afford to fall asleep because they needed to be gone long before another soldier came back to check on them.

« CHAPTER 13 »

Leon felt someone shaking him. "Come on, Leon! We fell asleep and we need to get out of here. I don't know what time it is and I'm afraid that soldier is going to come in and find us. Come on, Leon! Wake up!"

Leon moaned. "It's too cold to get up and I am nice and warm. Let me sleep a while longer."

Sam grabbed Leon's shoulder and shook harder. "Leon, we have to get out of this tent now! Can you understand what I am saying? We have to go now! That soldier is going to be coming in here at any time!"

Leon sat straight up. "Sam, we need to get out of here! If that soldier comes back and finds us we won't be able to get away. We must have fallen asleep. What time is it?" Leon asked as he scrambled to stand up. His ankle felt better, thank goodness, because he was afraid that they were going to have to make a run for it.

Sam didn't know whether to punch Leon on the shoulder or just answer the questions. He decided that he didn't have time to explain to Leon why he punched him so he just said, "I don't know what time it is. Let's see if we can go out through that tear that we saw last night."

They heard a noise that sounded like it was just outside the tent. They froze. Both of them held their breath so they wouldn't be heard. After a few seconds they heard the footsteps go away from the tent. They realized it was a guard that was patrolling the camp. They heard his footsteps as he walked on past the tent and further into the camp.

Sam motioned with his hands that he would crawl under the tent and that Leon would follow. Sam knelt down and saw that the tear was bigger than they thought. He pushed against the tent and the rip tore some more. It sounded like the noise of the rip ricocheted through the whole camp. He waited a couple seconds and then he tried again. This time he was able to slip out. He knew that Leon would not have any trouble because he was skinnier than Sam.

Sam waited while Leon got out. When Leon stood up he motioned that they should go to the right and follow the tree line out of the camp. Sam nodded in agreement and they went that direction.

The horses were tethered and lined up along a section of the trees. One of the horses nickered and snuffled. Sam heard what sounded like a hoof that scraped on the ground. He wondered if it was their horse, but he couldn't take the risk of the horse recognizing them. He was afraid that if the horse saw them he would make a loud enough noise to alert a guard. They continued along the tree line away from the horses. It seemed like they had been walking for an hour when it had only been a few minutes.

Leon turned to Sam and whispered, "I think we're clear of the camp. We should keep quiet until we are further away. We don't know how far away from the camp that they would have soldiers patrolling the area. We will continue in these trees and stay low."

Sam nodded in agreement. Sam thought to himself that he sure was glad that Leon was with him on this adventure. He wouldn't want to think what would have happened to him if he had been by himself.

They were still walking when the sun rose that morning. They had no idea where they were or which direction they were headed. All they knew to do was to keep walking.

Leon stopped suddenly. Sam nearly bumped into him. He had let his mind wander for a few minutes and he had not been paying attention. He must have missed something. "Leon, what's wrong? Did you hear something in the bushes?"

"Listen. It sounded like someone whistling. Someone is out there!"

Sam looked around. He let out a sigh of relief. "It's Henri. He found us! Come on."

"Henri!" Leon whispered loudly. "We're over here!"

Henri walked over to them. "Where have you been? I have been searching for you two. I was beginning to think that the soldiers had gotten you and kept you."

"It took us awhile but we found a hospital," Sam explained. "We saw a big building on a hill so we decided to walk to it to see if we could find food. A young girl gave us some food. We brought some for you and your family. We hope that it is enough."

"We do not eat very much so anything you brought will be plenty. Thank you for remembering us. Although, I will admit that your friend Billy built a snare and he caught a couple rabbits and even a squirrel. My mother made stew out of them so that has given us some nourishment. Now, we must get out of these woods. It will be completely light soon and we need to get back to the cave."

Sam and Leon followed Henri through the woods. They were so glad that Henri had found them. They were not sure that they would have found the cave again. And Billy was helpful? That was unusual...especially for Billy!

~~~

Billy met them at the opening of the cave. "Guys! I was beginning to get worried about you. Y'all have been gone for a while." He glanced over at Henri. "Henri and I have caught some small game to eat but I'm not sure how much longer we would be able to do that."

Sam felt embarrassed at the gratitude of Henri's family over the food that they had brought. It was only bread, cheese and apples. Anna had gathered them while he and Leon ate. It didn't seem like enough food for the three of them, but Henri said that it would last for several days. He, Leon and Billy would need to eat sparingly so the family would have more for themselves. He had never had to go without food before. It sure made him appreciate the meals that his mom cooked for their family. Even chicken nuggets sounded good right now.

Leon, Sam and Billy talked among themselves. They would need to see if they could find more food. Maybe they could look for a house nearby where they could ask for some. There was not enough food to feed six people for very long.

Sam wondered how long they would be in this time period. He had read about time travel but he couldn't remember how long it lasted. Surely someone had missed them by now.

Henri walked toward them. Sam asked Henri, "Do you think there is a house nearby where we could find some food? We want to help you and your family while we are here."

Henri replied, "I haven't seen any houses but I have stayed close to the woods. Perhaps if you go north there would be a small village. I know that my father spoke of a village that we would pass through. I have tried to stay close to the cave so my mother and sister would not be alone. It is my job to provide for them now but I don't know where to go by myself and I don't want to go too far away."

"Okay, we will go north and see if we can find a village. We don't know how long it will take us. Will you have enough food until we get back?" Leon asked.

"We will make the food go a long way. There will be enough for the three of us. Be careful and Godspeed."

Billy spoke up. "I want to stay here. I've been thinking that I want to try to make another snare and find a different place for it. Hopefully I can catch more small game. The food you brought will help but it will run out soon if Henri and his family have to stay much longer."

"Are you sure you want to stay behind, Billy? What if we can't find you again?" Sam asked.

"I'm sure. I mean, look, someone has to help them and I'm all they have right now."

~~~

Sam and Leon began to walk north. Once again they stayed near the trees and bushes and away from the road. They did not want any soldiers that came along the road to find them out in the open.

The weather had turned colder. Sam sure was glad they had the coats. He was like Leon in that he wasn't sure he liked the fur around his face, but now it felt good.

He had to admit that the long underwear under his pants was warm but they sure were itchy against his legs..

"Can you believe that Billy wanted to stay behind with Henri and his family? What will happen if we can't find our way back to him?" Leon asked Sam with a frown on his face.

"No, I can't believe that Billy wanted to stay behind and I don't really feel comfortable with his decision to do that. We will have to worry about finding him later. For now, let's just keep walking in this direction."

After they had been walking for a while, Leon nudged Sam in the ribs. "Look. There are some people walking around over there. Do you think that this is the village that Henri spoke about, although it doesn't really look like a village."

"I don't know. Let's hide in those bushes and watch for a while. We want to make sure that we aren't about to walk in on a soldier's camp. It will be dark soon so let's eat our bread that Henri gave us."

Darkness settled in. Sam and Leon huddled close together so that they could stay warm. This was not like the camping trip that Dad took them on last year. Then they used tents and sleeping bags. *And* they had a fire. Sam could see a fire in the distance and he could hear men talking but he could not hear what was being said.

Sam looked up at the sky. The stars seemed brighter than he had ever seen. There seemed to be a frostiness about the air…almost like it was before snow fell at home in Tennessee. They didn't get much snow at home, but Sam remembered that there was a frosty nip in the air just before a big snow.

"Sam! Wake up! We are not outside and there is a fire! Where are we?"

"Leon, you must be hallucinating. We were looking for a village and fell asleep under the tree. Remember?"

"Bonjour. Did you sleep well?"

Sam and Leon jumped up. Who was this man and where were they? Had they been captured by the soldiers?

The man who stood before them was tall and large. He had a mustache that had a slightly upward curl and kind eyes.

Sam was the first to speak. "Who are you?"

"I am Sir Edward Hulse, at your service," Sir Edward bowed slightly. "Now, young man, the question *is*, 'who are you' and where do you come from?"

"Sir, I am Sam and this is my best friend, Leon. We are from America."

"And why are you here in these woods at this particular time?" Sir Edward asked.

"We were visiting a friend. Henri. We got separated from him and we weren't sure how to find him," Sam replied.

Leon found his voice. "Yes sir. We were trying to find food for Henri and his mother and sister. You see, Henri's father has been captured and they need food real bad so Sam and I were trying to find a village to get them some food. They are in a cave...somewhere" (his voice dropped to a near whisper).

"Henri said that his father was captured by the Germans. You aren't German..." Sam gulped "...are you?"

Sir Edward belted out a hearty laugh. "No, Son, I am not German. I am British. Come. I will take you to the mess hall and get you something to eat. I'm sure you two are hungry."

They followed him out of what looked to be a trench that was dug in the ground. While walking Sam asked, "How did we get in there? I remember we were under some trees trying to stay warm. The stars were so bright and beautiful. Then I must have fallen asleep. And I think it snowed!"

"One of my men was doing patrol and he saw something under a tree. When he went to inspect what it was, he found the two of you huddled together. Yes, it snowed. In fact, when my officer found you, the two of you were already covered in a light snow. He couldn't very well leave you out there to freeze to death. Now could he?" Sir Edward replied.

"Sir, if you don't mind me asking, was that a ditch that we were in? It was a small space with dirt walls and floor." Sam asked Sir Edward.

"That 'ditch' you mentioned is what we call a trench. We built the trenches underground for protection. They usually have an embankment at the top and a barbed wire fence. Often the trenches are reinforced with sandbags and wooden beams. In the trench itself, the bottom is covered with wooden boards called duckboards. These boards help to protect the soldiers' feet from the water in the trenches."

Leon looked around the area. "Who built these trenches?" he asked.

Sir Edward paused. "The soldiers built the trenches. We basically had to build them as we went along the land. A lot of work had to be done at night so that we would not be seen by the enemy. It was a very slow process and we continue to build them as we go along enemy lines."

They continued to walk along the trench for a short distance. Sir Edward stopped and opened a door that was built into the side of the trench. There were a couple of small steps that lead down into the trench. There was a good aroma that filled the small area. Sam's stomach growled, which reminded him that he was hungry..

Sir Edward took them up to a long table. "Cook! These young men need to be fed. Be a good chap and take care of them for me. Make sure they eat heartily because this is a special night. After all, it is Christmas Eve."

"Christmas Eve?" Sam had lost track of time and did not realize that it was now December 24th.

Cook did a half salute to Sir Edward. "Yes sir! I will see to it that they eat. But before they eat at my table I expect them to wash their hands. And wash those faces and naked ears, too!" Cook barked at them.

Sam and Leon went to the wash bowl that Cook pointed out to them. Leon whispered, "What did he mean by 'wash your naked ears'? Aren't ears always naked?"

Sam chuckled. "I think he meant to say neck and ears. His accent made it hard to understand what he was saying. Let's get washed up and eat. I'm starving!"

Sam and Leon each took a biscuit. The meat was hard, kinda like beef jerky, and the jam was sweet. They ate quickly because they were hungry. They could hear Sir Edward and Cook talking but they could not make out what they were saying. Sam hoped that they could stay in this camp for a while, but not too long. He wanted to go home for Christmas.

After they finished eating Sir Edward took them back outside. "Boys, I don't know how you got here but I must tell you that you need to stay in the trenches until we decide what to do with you. Whatever you do, don't wander off. It would be too easy to go into "No Man's Land.""

Leon looked up at Sir Edward. "No Man's Land? What is that?"

Sam spoke up, "That's the space between the two enemy trench lines."

"And how would you know that, Lad? Are you a spy?" Sir Edward asked quietly.

Sam froze. He knew too much history from watching the History Channel on TV. What could he say to convince this soldier that he was not a spy. Sam began to stutter, "Well, sir, you see, uh, well, my grandfather fought in a war and he told me about the space that was called 'No Man's Land.'"

"Hm. That's interesting. Most young boys would not remember something like that. Are you sure that you aren't a spy?"

"Sir, I promise you that we are not spies. We are here visiting and we don't know anything about the war. I just have a great memory when it comes to history. In fact, history is my favorite subject in school." Sam was afraid that Sir Edward was going to make a big deal out of his statement. He could not make that mistake again. Sam would have liked to ask more questions about the trenches, but he was afraid that Sir Edward would think that he was trying to spy on them.

They continued walking for a bit. "Lads, I need to part company with you for now. I have some matters that I need to attend to. I will leave you in the hands of one of my soldiers. I suggest that you may want to get some rest. We don't usually get much sleep during the night because of the firing guns around us. Tomorrow we need to find a way to get you out of the camp and back to wherever you're supposed to be."

The boys went into the trench. They could hear a voice coming down the trench so they decided to check it out. They rounded a bend in the trench and came upon a man sitting at a table with a strange looking radio and microphone that he was talking into. He looked surprised when he saw Sam and Leon. "How can I help you lads?" he asked.

"Wow! This is a cool room!" both boys exclaimed. "I've never seen a radio like that before." Sam said.

"Well, I would be surprised if you had," the soldier quipped. "This radio is used to communicate with our airplanes in the area. They let us know what is going on in our area and where the enemy is located."

The radio squawked and squealed. The soldier turned his attention back to the radio. The person on the other end said something that the boys could not understand. The soldier replied, "Copy that, one-niner. I'll pass along the information."

The soldier clicked off the radio and said, "Lads, I need you to run along now. I have work to do."

Sam and Leon left the trench and went to find a place to rest.

~~~

They laid in the trench after a light snack. They could see the stars through the cracks in the roof. It was very peaceful in the camp at the moment.

Earlier in the evening the boys had heard gunfire. They had been frightened by the sounds of the guns, but one of the men explained that the shooting was a few miles away and that they would be safe as long as they stayed in the trench. They were worried for Billy and Henri. Did they have enough food or would they be caught in the crossfire of the fighting?

Suddenly there was a noise in the distance. It sounded like singing.

They could not understand the words but they recognized the tune. The men in the camp began to sing along as they all sang "Silent Night".

Sam looked at Leon. Leon looked at Sam. Both of them had tears in their eyes as they realized the significance of the moment.

Then they heard shouts of: "Joyeux Noël! Joyeux Noël!"

The Christmas Miracle of 1914

"Merry Christmas, Boys!" Sir Edward exclaimed!

"Merry Christmas, Sir Edward!" Sam and Leon sighed.

It was almost midnight on Christmas Eve. The damp weather had given way to the cold and a glistening frost had settled over yesterday's snow. Sam and Leon saw a tiny Christmas tree with candles that glowed in the bright moonlight. They wondered where it had come from.

Some of the men responded to the events of Christmas Eve. They tentatively emerged from their trenches into No Man's Land on Christmas Day. Enemy soldiers and allies met and spent Christmas together.

The men exchanged gifts of scarves, tobacco, cigarettes, cookies and candy from home. They took photos together to commemorate the occasion.

They had left the damp of the trenches and used the time of peace to tend to the dead and wounded. Some of the soldiers from both sides began a friendly game of football. It wasn't important who won the game...they just played to be friendly...even though they knew that it would only be for a short time.

Sir Edward, Sam and Leon watched the festivities from a distance. Sam remembered some of the history of this night from his internet research and the History Channel. He could not believe that he had just witnessed such a momentous piece of history.

He looked up at Sir Edward and noticed his calm features. Sam placed his hand on Sir Edward's arm. "This was the most magical night I have ever witnessed. Thank you for allowing Leon and me to be a part of the Christmas miracle of this truce."

Sir Edward put a hand on each boy's shoulder and squeezed gently. "This was indeed a magical night. It was a brief respite from all the ugliness of war. But I believe that the two of you, however you got here, were the real Christmas miracle during this truce.

"Through your eyes I could see Christmas like when I was a child. For just a few brief moments I was back at home with my mother and father, tearing open my presents without a care in the world. Thank you.

"Now, do you want your present?" Sir Edward teased with a glint in his eye.

"Sir, this was our present!" Sam exclaimed as he spread out his arms to indicate the men before him. "There is no need to give us anything more."

"I agree!" Leon said somberly.

"Come along. I think you're going to like this present." Sir Edward turned and walked ahead of them while the boys practically ran to keep up with him..

When they arrived at the trench where they had spent the night, Sir Edward opened the flap and motioned for the boys to go inside.

"Merry Christmas!" Shouted Henri.

Sam and Leon just stared. There was Henri with his mother and sister. And Billy!

"How…how did you get here?" Leon exclaimed.

"Sir Edward sent some men to find us. They came just in time because we had run out of food. We have been fed and we will stay in the camp until my father is found. Thank you, Sam and Leon, for making this the best Christmas ever!"

They visited with Henri and his mother and sister for a few more minutes.

As Sam, Leon and Billy left the trench with Sir Edward, they heard a strange noise. Sir Edward shielded his eyes as he looked toward the sky. "Look boys! A plane is flying over."

Sam looked up toward the sky. He could see the plane coming toward them. "We need to take cover!" Sam yelled to Leon. "That plane is going to shoot at us!"

"Shoot us? I can't be shot! I need to get home," Leon said in a panicked voice.

"Whoa there, Boys! You don't need to go anywhere. This isn't a fighter plane. It's a military observation plane. It is used to locate enemy lines and to gather information from the air. We refer to it as a 'reconnaissance role' for the pilot." Sir Edward explained. "Let's watch to see what the pilot will do."

The three boys stood with Sir Edward and watched as the plane flew closer to them. They could see the white scarf tied around the pilot's throat and how it blew in the wind behind him. Suddenly the plane came closer to the ground and waggled its wings at them. The boys fell backwards onto the ground when they saw the underbelly of the plane as it roared over their heads.

The dawn's early sunrise caused a bright reflection on the wings of the plane. That was the last thing they saw as they heard a faint voice call out "Merry Christmas!"

CHAPTER 14

Back to the Present

Sam opened his eyes and looked around. He was in the library! Where were Leon and Billy? Did they make it back with him? The last thing he remembered was a plane had flown over them.

"Hey you guys! Mom sent me to find you. What have y'all been doing back here?" Sophie asked.

She picked up the chair that had been turned over when Sam tried to put the brass box on the shelf. She retrieved the box from under the table where it had slid when Sam fell from the chair. She handed it to Sam but he gently laid it on top of the table, refusing to attempt another reach for the top shelf.

Sam looked at Leon. Leon looked at Sam.

They grabbed each other and shouted, "We're back! We're back!" They slapped each other on the back.

"What are you shouting about? You act as though you have been gone for a week. It's only been twenty minutes, but long enough for Mom to get worried. I have to get back out there but y'all need to get out there, too."

Sam jumped up and down. "We saw the Christmas Truce of 1914! We witnessed history in the making! No one is ever going to believe us! How can we even explain this?" Sam's words tumbled over each other in his excitement.

Leon grabbed Sam's arm. "Dude! You can't tell anybody about this! People will think you have gone nuts. Nope! This will have to be our secret till the day we die." Leon said soberly.

Sam stopped jumping. He began to pace the floor. What was he thinking? Of course they could not tell anyone. History had been written. If they told anyone that they had witnessed the Christmas Truce of 1914 it could alter the history books.

"You're right, Leon. This will be our secret. I'm so glad that we experienced that time together." Sam said with resignation.

Billy stood there with a look of awe on his face. "I don't know what to think about what we experienced. I mean, we, just witnessed a historical moment in history! I have never liked history lessons before, but now I can't wait to learn more about it. Sam, I owe you an apology for all the times that I called you 'Mr. History'. I promise to do better. In fact, do you think you could do some tutoring with me? I need to get better grades in school."

"Billy, it would be my honor to tutor you. I'm glad you went with us, too, to witness the Christmas Truce of 1914. While we can't talk about it with anyone, I believe that our lives have been changed for the better."

"I know you like to play basketball, Sam, but do you think that you would want to come over to my house to pitch a baseball around sometime? My dad and I pitched a lot before he died...in fact, my dad was a great baseball player. He had trophies from his high school days."

"Wow. I didn't know that about your dad. I would like that, Billy. Even though baseball is not my favorite sport, I have played a little. I can probably remember enough to play catch with you.."

"That would be great. I think it would be good for my mom to see that I have friends. And, you can even bring Leon with you...if you think he can play catch," Billy said with a laugh and a twinkle in his eyes.

"Well, he can't catch as well as he can dribble, but I think he would like that, too." Sam grinned as he punched Billy on the arm.

~~~

The play was a huge success. Mr. Teddy sat front and center of the stage. Sam studied his face from behind the curtain. He appeared to be mesmerized by everything that unfolded in front of him.

Beth explained to the audience that her grandfather was there and that his father, Mack Sampson, had fought in World War I. She showed the sword that Mack had found. Then she invited Mr. Teddy up to the stage.

As Mr. Teddy stood on the stage, he expressed his thoughts, "I cannot tell you what this play has done for me. It brought great joy to me as I envisioned my daddy fighting in that war. Beth and all my grandchildren called my daddy 'MackDaddy'. They loved to spend time with him just as he loved spending time with them. He loved to tell them stories of how it was when he was young.

"They never knew about his war experiences until the last year of his life. He couldn't talk about that time because it was too painful. This play brought out good and bad things that happened in that war. The Christmas Truce of 1914 was special to all the soldiers of that time. It was special to their families, too. So many of the soldiers sent letters home to tell their families about that event. Some of those letters are still around today. Thank goodness some people thought to preserve that significant time in history."

Mr. Teddy paused for a moment to wipe tears from his eyes. He looked over the crowd until he spotted Sam and Leon. "I would like to share some information that is not known to many. I found the information in a small-town library many years ago when I visited England. A soldier had written home to tell his family about the Christmas Truce. I will never forget what he wrote. It went something like this…"

Dear Ma,

> *I cannot begin to tell you what a great Christmas I had even though I was in the trenches of war. There was a short truce where soldiers from both sides played kickball and even exchanged small gifts: tobacco, a scarf, cigarettes, homemade cookies and candy that were sent from home. It was a grand ol' time, even for a few short hours. But, Ma, the best part was these two young lads who witnessed this event. Sam and*

Leon were in our camp because they needed to find food for a family that was living in a cave. These are hard times, Ma, that have been made magical because two young lads gave of themselves. Sir Edward Hulse was overheard to say that those boys were the 'Christmas Miracle during this Truce of 1914.' I have to close my letter now. The war has resumed, but if I survive this war, I will always fondly remember Christmas 1914.'

Love, Your Son...

"Interestingly enough that letter was not signed. It was from a young soldier who needed to let his mother know that he was okay. We don't know what happened to that young man, but I'm so glad we have his letter, and others like it, even today."

Beth and some of the young men helped Mr. Teddy off the stage after a thunderous standing ovation. There was not a dry eye in the house. Mr. Teddy sat back down in his seat as many well-wishers gathered around him to shake his hand and speak to him for a few minutes.

~ ~ ~

Sam and Leon waited patiently near the stage until everyone had finished talking with Mr. Teddy before they went over to speak to him.

"Do you have to go home tomorrow, Mr. Teddy?" Sam asked sadly.

"It's time for me to leave. I cannot tell you boys how much I have enjoyed the time I spent with you. Especially you, Sam." Mr. Teddy paused, his Adam's apple bobbed up and down as he tried to overcome his emotions. "Stay interested in history, Sam. Your insight on some of the things we discussed was amazing. You can never know too much history. I know your parents are very proud of you. Both of you. I know that I am proud of you.

"Now, Lads," Mr. Teddy exclaimed with a wink and a nod, "don't try to alter the history books."

Mr. Teddy laughed and motioned for Beth. She came over with a package in her hand. Mr. Teddy unwrapped the package. Sam recognized the sword. "Sam, I have talked with Beth, and she and I have agreed that we want you to have Mack's sword. With your passion for history, we know that it will be safe with you."

Sam took a step backward. "Mr. Teddy, I cannot accept that sword. It belongs in your family. I mean, I appreciate your generous offer, but I have to refuse."

"Sam, it would mean so much to me if you would accept it. No one in my family has shown any interest in the sword or the story behind it. I know that if you have the sword, Mack's story will live on for generations. So, please, do this old man a favor and accept it with my blessing."

Mr. Teddy handed the sword to Sam. Sam looked at it in his hands. He raised tear-filled eyes to Mr. Teddy. Then he laid the sword on Mr. Teddy's lap, threw his arms around his neck and hugged him with all his might. "Mr. Teddy, I will be honored to accept Mack's sword. I will never let his story die and I will never forget you!"

"And I will never forget you, Sam. Now here, take your sword and run along. Godspeed young man!"

Sam took the sword from Mr. Teddy. He looked up to see that older man's eyes were damp. He stepped back. Beth came over and helped Mr. Teddy from his seat and they walked out the door.

Sam looked at Leon with disbelief. "Leon, do you think Mr. Teddy knew that we witnessed the Christmas Truce of 1914? But how could he know?"

Leon pondered this question a few moments. His eyes misted over as he thought about what they had seen. Then he nudged Sam in the ribs and declared, "Naw! How could anyone know about that? It's going to be our secret. Remember?"

Sam put his arm around Leon's shoulder as they took one last look at the old theater. "You're right, Leon! It's gotta be our secret."

The boys walked out into the night. Leon's arm around Sam's shoulder as Sam carried the sword.

About the Authors

Kannon E. Graves is a grandson to Kathleen Graham-Gandy. He lives with his parents and sister in southern Middle Tennessee where he is a sixth grader. Kannon loves history…in fact, his fifth grade history teacher often let Kannon explain historical events, especially for World War I and World War II. He loves to play football and basketball. He has played both sports since second grade. When Kannon asked his Mewaw to help him write a book about WWI, she readily agreed to help him.

Mack Graves, Kannon's grandfather, is called 'MackDaddy' by his grandchildren. Kannon wanted to honor his grandfather by using his name as a character in this book.

Kathleen Graham-Gandy, a retired banker, has always had the desire to write. Her writing experiences include training manuals for bank loan officers, and as a journalist for a local newspaper. She loves going into local schools to share with students about history in her local area. Graham-Gandy is the author of three books: "Mount Pleasant's 100 South Main Street;" "One Man's Vision…One County's Reward," (How the life of James H. Stribling Affected His Fellow Man); and "Shock Therapy!" (Building a Power Line with a Blonde Groundman).

Graham-Gandy was honored when her grandson showed interest in becoming an author. She and her husband, Charles, make their home in Middle Tennessee.

38510755R00087

Made in the USA
Middletown, DE
13 March 2019